ESCAPE!

ESCAPE!

SIGURD SENJE

TRANSLATED FROM THE NORWEGIAN BY EVELYN RAMSDEN

A VOYAGER BOOK

HARCOURT, BRACE & WORLD, INC., NEW YORK

Originally published in Norway in 1961 by N. W. Damm & Søn
under the title *Stepans Skrin*

Library of Congress Catalog Card Number: 64-12509
Printed in the United States of America

Contents

CONTENTS

ESCAPE!

1 — The Box and the War

The box in this story is a souvenir from World War II. It is of shining metal covered with strange patterns and inscriptions, and it stands on the mantelpiece in a peaceful little house on the coast of Norway as a reminder of a time when there was no peace.

This foreign-looking souvenir was made by Stepan, a Russian prisoner of war in Norway. He made it as two boxes that could be fitted together so that they looked like one. This was Stepan's own idea, and he had his own secret reason for doing it.

The secret reason was a pair of young Norwegians who were his friends, so the story of Stepan's box is their very own story. Their names were Ingrid and Elling, and they were both about fourteen years old when the war reached that part of the coast where they lived. They were in the same class in school and lived in the same house, and they had been devoted to each other ever since they were both six years old. In time they would probably marry.

Their families each lived in a separate part of the same house, and both their fathers were officers in the merchant marine and were mostly away at sea on long voyages.

9

They were at sea when the frontiers in Norway were closed by the Germans, so that they could not get home. Happily the two mothers were good friends and kept each other company in their loneliness.

Ingrid's and Elling's homes were so peaceful and out of the way that they hardly noticed when the war swept in over Norway on April 9, 1940. They knew nothing of the German invasion except for the noise of planes high overhead and the smoke from ships out at sea. They did not realize that the ships were warships or that the planes carried bombs to be dropped on targets in Norway. They read about the German spring campaign in the papers and heard about it on the radio.

When the Norwegian troops had been forced to give in and there was no more news about shooting, their home became as quiet and peaceful as ever. It rained a great deal that summer; otherwise, it was like all other summers along the coast. People bathed, tried their luck at fishing, and when the weather was fine, they went on family trips to the surrounding islands.

But by degrees the fuel for these pleasure boats decreased and then was very strictly rationed. It was needed for military purposes, and only those who had to have it for professional use were allowed to buy a gallon or two at a time. Oars and sails came into fashion again.

It was, of course, holiday time for Ingrid and Elling, and they sailed among the little islands off the coast as usual. Now and again a German destroyer or a motor torpedo boat rushed up the fjord, and when Ingrid and Elling went into the nearby town, they saw German soldiers and sailors in the streets. These strangers aroused curiosity for a time, but they became a familiar sight and people grew accustomed to seeing them. Soon no one even looked up when the planes with the swastika painted beneath their wings droned in the sky above them. Norway was occupied by the Germans, but this did not affect the calm stream of daily life in Ingrid and Elling's remote part of the country—not yet.

It was not until the autumn that anything began to happen. Then a stiff-lipped German officer from the German coast artillery appeared and wanted just this particular spot as a shooting range. Away with the families living there—the military must be first and foremost!

All the houses had to be evacuated within two weeks, and their owners had to find other accommodations as best they could.

Most of the people managed pretty well, for in difficult times people are always eager to help one another. The homeless found shelter with their relations or with kind people living in the neighborhood or further up country.

The two seafaring families had to go far afield. Ingrid's mother came from a farm in the Gudbrand Valley, an inland farming district, and she and Ingrid moved there. She found lodgings for her old friend on another farm in the same district, so Elling and his mother moved there, too. Then the two young people were neighbors again and in the same class at school, but this time in the senior school.

A year passed. It was impossible to get fresh fish from the sea up there in the valley; otherwise, there was not much to complain about during that winter. The next winter things were worse. There was great cold, lack of food, stronger pressure from the Germans; all radios were forbidden; there were shocking announcements about the executions of Norwegians.

Toward the end of this miserable winter of 1942, a man named Stepan came to Norway as a prisoner of war from the Eastern Front, with a few thousand more of his fellow countrymen. They had been taken prisoner by German troops in the Ukraine, and the victors now sent them to Norway—and to other occupied countries—to work for them there.

Stepan came to the Gudbrand Valley in a detachment of fifty men. They had traveled all the long way from Russia herded together like cattle in trucks and on cargo ferries. They had had practically no food and were all starving, completely exhausted, and dirty. Their guards drove them at the double from the station into a camp, where they lived under canvas surrounded by high barbed-wire fencing. Here they were each given a little cabbage soup and one woolen blanket between two men. They had to sleep lying close together and fully dressed to avoid freezing to death in the tents.

Next morning they were sent—still at the double—into a wood, where they began building a road and digging a site for their own barracks. German guards carrying rifles saw that they did not have much rest. They worked as long as it was light and were each given a metal bowl full of cabbage soup at midday. For breakfast and supper they each had a piece of dry bread and water. Anyone who did not work hard was not given any food.

As most of them were young and strong and accustomed to hard work in their homeland, they managed to survive, but several of them fell ill after a time, and others died from ill-treatment and bad conditions.

Stepan was not young, but he was as strong as a horse and held out well during the first month. Swinging spades and hoes for a whole working day was not a joke when one's stomach was squeaking with hunger. But if they did not swing their tools fast enough, they were always dealt a blow across their shoulders from a German rifle butt or a kick in the back of their legs from a German soldier's boot.

Now and again a food parcel found its way in to them from the people living in the village. That was, of course, a great help for a day, but only for a day.

Throughout the spring, as the snow disappeared and the first green shoots came up from the ground, Stepan and his comrades were able to supplement their diet from nature. They ate grass and roots, clover and the juicy buds on the trees just as animals do. Even an occasional earthworm made a change in the green food, for a starving man does not mind very much what he eats.

But the Germans said, "Look at the Russians. They are no better than animals! They eat grass and earth."

The prisoners' stomachs swelled up on this diet, their

cheeks also, so that from the outside they did not look so bad. But under their uniforms they were only skin and bones.

In spite of this, Stepan had enough surplus energy to occupy himself with a hobby during the long, light spring evenings. He was a master in the art of fashioning metal articles and engraving patterns on them. This was a very ancient art in the place from which he came, and both his father and his grandfather had instructed him in it. Stepan himself had a son to whom he had taught the art.

At home in the Ukraine, Stepan had been trained as a technician and had held a good position in a factory. In the Red Army he was a technical officer in an engineering corps. Here in the Gudbrand Valley he had to dig just like all the others, but in the evenings he devoted himself to his art. He cut all sorts of things out of metal bowls and broken saucepans—from teaspoons to candlesticks and cigarette holders—and he engraved flower patterns on them and other charming designs.

He gave the finished articles to his fellow prisoners and to Norwegians who had smuggled food in to them. A few of the guards also secretly ordered souvenirs from Stepan. They paid him with extra food or tobacco.

Ingrid and Elling took parcels to the Russian camp as often as they could. Even if they themselves had worse food than they were accustomed to, they realized that things were much harder for the prisoners than for them. They soon learned enough German to talk to the sentries, and after a time many of the German soldiers managed to stammer out fairly good Norwegian.

Some of the sentries were stiff and unbending, but most of them turned a blind eye to the smuggling. If no officers were in the neighborhood, they would turn their backs when a Norwegian food parcel flew through the air to the nearest prisoner, who, of course, received it as a gift from the gods.

The schoolchildren generally did this job better than the grownups. If some cross-grained soldier chased Elling away, he never refused Ingrid, for Ingrid was as fair-haired and blue-eyed as she could be, and none of the soldiers could resist her for a moment.

As a matter of fact, there were others beside the German soldiers who looked long at Ingrid. She began to notice it herself, and now and again she made Elling jealous, sometimes on purpose but generally without meaning to do so.

But there was no place for romance among the prisoners themselves; it was the food they were after. Only Stepan, who made the little thank-you gifts for the givers, thought there was something special about the teen-age couple who stood outside the camp and waved to him. He looked at them with the eyes of an artist. However hungry he was, he never lost his feeling for the beauty and life around him. The sight of the two fair-haired young people strengthened his inspiration.

He was anxious to show them a little extra gratitude. One day he asked Willie, the kindliest of the sentries, to greet them for him and say that if they continued to be such special friends, he would make them a fine present— almost a wedding present. He would make it in such a

15

way that it would always remind them that they both belonged to each other.

Stepan would not say anything more about this present, but Willie knew that the prisoner had managed to find a damaged aluminum saucepan and that by degrees it was beginning to look like a box. It would take Stepan many weeks to make it, thought Willie, for he took as much trouble over it as if the gift were meant for a royal pair of lovers.

Ingrid and Elling asked Willie to tell Stepan that they meant to be married—that was a promise—and that his gift should stand in the middle of the wedding table.

When Stepan heard this, his busy hands began to work more eagerly than ever in the evenings.

In the meantime, his two young friends talked a great deal about what the present could possibly look like if it were to remind them of—no, that seemed too serious a subject even to discuss.

Then something happened that gave them other things to think about.

2 — Captain Schnell

A serious misfortune happened to Stepan—he fell ill.
When a Russian prisoner was sick, he was not allowed a
doctor; his companions had to look after him, and he
was often obliged to go out and dig and hoe as usual. Only
when he was so ill that he could not possibly stand was
he excused from work.

Because Stepan was very popular, things might not have
been so bad for him if something else had not happened
just before he fell sick. The commandant of the camp was
changed. The old commandant was sent to the Eastern
Front, and a new and much stricter one came in his place.
His name was Captain Schnell.

The old one had not paid much attention to his prisoners
but left them to his second-in-command and other sub-
ordinate officers. But Captain Schnell was the type of
commandant who wished to have a finger in every pie and
decide everything himself, both small and large matters.
He personally inspected the prisoners while they were
working and also in the evening in the sleeping quarters
that they had built for themselves.

People passing noticed the difference in the German

17

sentries. The soldiers hit and kicked the prisoners more than ever and shouted roughly if any one of them rested on his spade for a single moment. If an officer was in view, and particularly Captain Schnell, the prisoners were hit and kicked as if they had committed the worst possible offense.

The sentries were no longer willing to let in food parcels. Only Willie was as ready and unafraid as before.

But still no one refused Ingrid. When she approached, with her long fair hair and her roguish smile, all the German soldiers melted immediately and did all they could to please her. She was soon busy smuggling in everybody's parcels.

Captain Schnell almost never accepted the fact that a prisoner was ill. Illness was only an excuse for laziness, he said. If a prisoner could not work, neither should he eat. No cabbage soup for the sick, he commanded. During the first month that he was commandant, two prisoners died from hunger and exhaustion and a third was "shot during an attempted escape" as it was called—that is to say the guards chased him out into the forest and shot him in the back.

Stepan collapsed and lay restlessly on his bed for a couple of days, but then he had to get up and go to work as usual. He was bent almost double as he walked and looked ten years older, thought his Norwegian friends. When he saw Ingrid and Elling, he straightened himself up and tried to smile and wave to them as usual, but he could not really manage it. They realized that things were worse with him than they had thought.

A few days later they realized something else—that Captain Schnell had taken a personal dislike to Stepan and had made him the scapegoat of the camp.

After school that day Ingrid and Elling had hidden behind some trees, and they saw the commandant say something to one of the soldiers and point at Stepan. The soldier immediately ran forward and hit the prisoner over the back with his rifle, shouting at him, "Hurry, you lazy lout!"

Why had Captain Schnell given this order? He had no real grounds for it. But from then on Stepan was hit and kicked every day during the commandant's round.

Stepan grew worse quickly. He had greater difficulty than ever in walking and was not much use as far as the work was concerned. His young friends saw this, but what could they do? They tried to make plans to get him away and safely across the border to Sweden. They spoke to Willie about it, too, for they suspected that Willie and several of the other German sentries secretly hated Captain Schnell, but Willie shook his head.

"I might as well run away myself," he said. "To help a Russian prisoner to escape means death to a German soldier."

"But don't you want to go to Sweden, too?" asked the young people. "Aren't you sick of the war?"

Then Willie laughed loudly and noisily and answered that the stupid Norwegians might perhaps tempt him to do various things but not to desert. He was a loyal soldier in Hitler's army and would remain so as long as the war lasted.

So they had to try to get help somewhere else, for it was urgent.

Full of desperate energy, they discussed all possible and impossible solutions. The prospects were not bright and hope sank with each day, but the thought of freeing Stepan had sunk so deeply into their hearts that they could not enjoy anything until they had tried all possible ways.

3 — Jensen

One evening Elling had an unexpected visitor. Jensen, the telegraph clerk and assistant stationmaster, knocked at the door and asked him to come outside for a moment.

It was now late autumn—November—so it was pitch dark on the road, but Jensen drew Elling a few steps into the forest so that they could talk together there rather than in the open.

"I understand that you and Ingrid are planning to help Stepan to escape," he said.

"N-n-no. That's not true," stammered Elling. He did not know Jensen particularly well and so did not dare to confide in him straight off.

Jensen laughed, his white teeth gleaming in the dark. "I know what you are thinking," he said. "It's all right. I, too, am a good friend of Stepan's. He has made me a lovely cigarette holder. The Russian prisoners sawed up the winter wood for the station this year as perhaps you know."

"Yes, I know! Stepan was there!" Elling's voice was no longer suspicious.

"Well then, I have met Stepan and know what a valu-

21

able person he is," continued Jensen. "I cannot look on calmly and see him beaten to death by those German beasts or be made a target for that monster Captain Schnell's bad temper. I have a plan. I can't tell you any more about it at present, but I need help from both you and Ingrid. Can you keep a secret, both of you?"

By now Elling was so excited that he was perspiring, although he was standing out in the cold without a coat.

"Yes," he muttered thickly, "and you can depend on Ingrid just as well as on me. We would do anything in the world to save Stepan."

"Play truant from school even?"

"Of course!"

"Good," said Jensen. "I need you because you are both so young. You would not rouse the same suspicions, nor would you risk as much as we grownups. The Germans have not begun to shoot sixteen-year-olds—as yet."

"Th-that's obvious," said Elling, and shivered, although he was perspiring.

Jensen lowered his voice still more.

"Now listen carefully, Elling. The first thing you have to do is to go to your friend Willie the sentry and ask him three questions: The first, what would happen to the other prisoners if Stepan escaped. Have you understood?"

"What will happen to the other prisoners if Stepan escaped," repeated Elling glibly.

"Second, which night he will be on guard next in the camp."

"Which night he will be on guard next."

22

"Third, is he willing to get a dent in his steel helmet for Stepan's sake?"

"A dent in . . ." Elling stopped. He did not know whether he had understood rightly.

"No more questions. He'll understand. Repeat!"

"Is he willing to get a dent in his helmet?" Elling repeated. Jensen cleared his throat, satisfied.

"Now you must go and explain the whole thing to Ingrid and then report Willie's answers to me at the station tomorrow at four o'clock. Come by yourself. Is that clear?"

"Clear. Tomorrow at four o'clock."

"Fine. Good night, Elling."

"Good night, Jensen."

4 — It's Urgent

Next day, a quarter of an hour before the appointed time, Elling rushed up the hill to the station. There everything was locked and quiet, but he saw Jensen sitting at his desk in the office and knocked on the windowpane.

Jensen let him in, locked the door behind him, and scolded him for coming too early.

"When I say four o'clock, I mean four o'clock," he said.

"But you know—it's very urgent about Stepan!" panted Elling. "Today Ingrid and I saw—"

"One moment," Jensen interrupted quietly. "The report first. What did our friend Willie answer? Take the questions in the right order please."

"All right! It took me a long time to find Willie, for he was not on guard. Finally I found him over in the café."

"Fine. What did he answer?"

"Well, to question one Willie answered that he did not think Captain Schnell would kill any of the other prisoners if Stepan got away. Not to begin with at any rate, he said, for the commandant would move heaven and earth to catch Stepan. He takes a special pleasure in tormenting and plaguing Stepan, just Stepan and no one else. And he has said that he will himself shoot 'that damned artist' one of these days. Shoot him in the neck. Isn't it awful?"

"Hmm," growled Jensen, "just as I thought. That isn't too bad for us. And then the next answer?"

"Willie is not on guard until next Thursday night," said Elling disconsolately, "and today is only Monday. But I can't understand—"

"I'll explain everything to you later on," Jensen interrupted. "What was the answer to the last question?"

Elling looked down on the floor.

"Willie said no. He didn't feel inclined to spoil his steel helmet."

"That I also expected, but he'll soon feel inclined to do so. Do you think *we* can make him agree to it, Elling?"

"N-n-no, I don't think so."

"Not even if we ask Ingrid to help us?"

Elling blushed up to the roots of his hair.

"I—I didn't think of that."

Jensen laughed. "I have been a soldier myself, and I know soldiers. Where girls are concerned, they agree to everything, and with the greatest of pleasure! To be hit on the head with an iron rod will only be fun."

Elling stared at him doubtfully.

"Is—is Ingrid to hit him?"

Jensen did not answer. He put on a glove, opened a cupboard, and took out a short broken-off bit of iron piping. It was once part of the braking machinery of a freight

25

car, he explained. It had been wiped clear of fingerprints, and no one must grasp it with his bare hands, an important thing to remember! He swung the broken piping in the air.

"Don't you think that this weapon would make a good dent in a steel helmet?" he asked, laughing. "I think so, at any rate. Now go to Ingrid with it and ask her to hide it carefully. No one else must get the slightest glimpse of it. Understood?"

"Understood."

"And no fingerprints on it as I have said."

"No fingerprints."

"She can train herself on a large head of cabbage. And tomorrow she must report to me that Willie is willing. That's a fine rhyme, Willie is willing, isn't it?"

Elling stood there twisting and turning and did not answer at once.

"Say yes," commanded Jensen good-naturedly.

"Yes, Jensen," came meekly from Elling.

"Four o'clock, precisely! Got it?"

"Precisely, Jensen."

"Good. And now we come to you, Elling, and the job that you are to do. You look very glum. Are you jealous?"

"N-n-no." Elling blushed over his whole face. He hastened to add, "It's just that there is such a hurry with Stepan."

"Exactly. Now you can tell me why."

And then Elling told him how he and Ingrid had once more hidden themselves to spy on Captain Schnell when he inspected the prisoners as they worked. The young people had knelt behind a bush where they could see everything without being seen. The first thing they noticed was that Stepan was more bent than ever and was dragging his spade. He dug only a few spadefuls and was obliged to rest. When the commandant came to him, he tried to pull himself together and pretend that he was perfectly well. He took one or two quick, powerful spadefuls like the others, but then he had to bend over and rest again. Captain Schnell bawled something to the guard, and the guard began to belabor Stepan with the butt of his rifle. One of the blows made the prisoner stumble, and he fell on his face on the ground. The soldier continued to kick and hit him where he lay. Stepan tried to pull himself onto his legs again. His face was covered with earth and dirt. He got to his feet but tottered, and the soldier gave him another heavy blow with the butt of his rifle and kicked him on his shins.

Then Stepan began to weep. The great, powerful man sobbed as if he were a child, helplessly and uncontrollably. Ingrid and Elling, kneeling behind the bush, could not stay there any longer. They squeezed each other's hands and slipped away. Captain Schnell's Prussian voice cut through Stepan's weeping, and they heard him say distinctly, *"Er ist bald fertig"*—"He's almost done for."

Elling's voice thickened as he told his story.

"So you see it is very urgent," he muttered at last.

Jensen wrinkled his forehead and thoughtfully tapped the cigarette holder Stepan had made on the table. "Hitler and his race-madness!" he shouted suddenly aloud. "Stepan is a Slav, and for Hitler only Germans are human beings!"

Then he lowered his voice again. "Ask Ingrid to try to persuade Willie to tell Stepan that he must hold out until Thursday."

"All right, Jensen."

"We can't ask Willie to change his sentry duty, as then he may bring suspicion on himself, and we can't use anyone except Willie."

"No," answered Elling. "We don't know any of the other soldiers well enough."

Jensen put a cigarette stub into his holder and finished smoking it in a few furious puffs. The stink of homemade tobacco floated about the office. He dropped the last little bit of cigarette into the ashtray and looked at Elling sharply.

"And now at last we come to your job, Elling. You are ready to do anything, you said?"

"Anything in the world, Jensen."

"And your mother will not object?"

"Not if it means saving Stepan."

"All right then. Feel your ear. It's very painful, isn't it?" Once again Elling did not understand, but he had begun to get used to Jensen, so he obediently lifted his hand to his ear and began feeling it.

"If you want it to hurt, then it will hurt," he answered.

"Fine," said Jensen satisfied, "for tonight you are going to have the most violent earache of your life. It will be so bad that you will have to be sent to the hospital in town tomorrow."

"But—but what in the world will they say there?" asked Elling, feeling quite confused.

"Now keep calm. You are asking too many questions. The hospital is your alibi as far as the neighbors and the Germans are concerned, you understand. Everyone will think of you as safely tucked up in bed there, but in reality you will not go farther away than here to this station. Is that clear?"

"Yes."

"My room is your hospital. You will stay here until Thursday. Bring a toothbrush and your food ration cards with you, and an extra passport photo, as well as your identity card. You will have further instructions later. Is that clear?"

"Clear," answered Elling firmly. Now at last he began to glimpse a meaning in the whole affair.

5 — Top Secret

Tuesday, Wednesday, and Thursday were hard waiting days for Stepan and tedious days for his rescuers.

On Tuesday Ingrid came up to the station to report to Jensen exactly at four o'clock. She told him that she had talked for a long time with Willie the evening before, trying to persuade him to help. She had had to be extra sweet and loving to him, and they had walked up and down for some time, hand in hand. To begin with, Willie had said the same to her as he had said to Elling, namely that he could not, as a German soldier, help a Russian prisoner of war to escape. But she had joked and teased him and worked him up against Captain Schnell; yes, she had even cried real tears for Stepan's sake, and finally Willie had agreed. She had made him understand that the escape plan that had been worked out was not going to depend on him. As a sentry, he would risk nothing. He was not allowed, naturally, to know who was behind the plan.

"Splendid, Ingrid," Jensen growled in agreement. "I must say you are pretty smart. I knew you would bring it off."

"Oh, it wasn't so bad," said Ingrid shyly. "Elling would have done it just as well if he had been a girl."

"Obviously." Jensen smiled. "Your Elling is a fine boy, but I heard he has a very bad earache today."

"It began yesterday. It's such a bad case that he has to go to the hospital today to be examined."

"That's sensible of him. Which train is he catching?"

"The evening train."

"The evening train. Yes, that's excellent."

Ingrid looked up at Jensen.

"Elling will be all right in the hospital, won't he?"

"In the hospital, yes! I can guarantee you that." Jensen laughed so loudly that the windowpanes clattered.

Ingrid also laughed, but more carefully. She was longing to know a little more about the plan, but Jensen only explained to her what she herself was to do, not a single syllable more—exactly as he had done to Elling.

None of the people taking part in the plan must know more than was absolutely necessary. This he impressed on her. It was important in case any one of them should fall into the hands of the Germans. Everyone who was interrogated by the Gestapo, and perhaps tortured with a glowing cigarette end pressed against his skin, with thumb screws, or with any of the other devilish instruments, must not know too much. He might all too easily betray the whole.

Ingrid understood this immediately. Elling, on his side, knew nothing more than that he was to go to the hospital.

After this Ingrid asked Jensen no more questions, but she told him that things had not been any better for Stepan today. He was surrounded by blows and kicks and shouted threats, although anyone could see that the man should

31

really be in bed, that he ought not to have to work. She hoped earnestly that Willie would be able to speak to him fairly soon so that he knew this torture would not go on forever.

"I hope so, too!" said Jensen and clenched his fists.

When Wednesday came, it really did seem as if Stepan had acquired new strength. He was still obviously ill and weak, but his face did not look quite so old and defeated and he was not quite so bent as the day before.

Captain Schnell noticed it, and it did not please him. Rather the contrary, for he barked and raged more hoarsely than usual and made the guards use their rifle butts on Stepan without the slightest provocation. He even took hold of his own pistol and fired a shot right over the head of the prisoner.

That Wednesday the village people heard that Elling had an earache and had gone to the hospital on Tuesday evening. No one paid much attention to that. Anyone might have an earache, and it often happened that people went to Oslo to see the specialist. Besides, Elling was only a guest here in the district and not known to many.

Elling had gone with his mother to catch the evening train. It was pitch dark on the road, and there were only weak blue lamps in the station. The few travelers on the platform could hardly recognize each other in this light. Besides, most of them were Germans in uniform.

The train came—very late as was usual in wartime— and Elling climbed on board. He waved good-by to his mother and shut the train door after him. His mother turned around immediately and went home. The acting stationmaster, Jensen, wearing a red band around his cap, signaled "All clear" to the guard, the guard blew his whistle and waved his green lamp toward the engine, the engine driver gave a short blast with the steam whistle, and the train moved slowly out of the station.

All went calmly and normally, and only Jensen remained on the empty platform laughing to himself in the half darkness. No one had noticed that one of the passengers, a boy of high school age, had behaved rather strangely. Instead of finding himself a place, he went straight across the corridor and out on the other side of the train. There he was engulfed by the darkness and did not return, but when Jensen, a little later, entered his office in the station building, he found Elling there.

"Here I am," said Elling, handing him an envelope, "and here is my butter card, bread card, and meat card, and the photograph you asked me for."

"Fine," said Jensen, "welcome to the hospital."

The time of waiting began.

Elling sat in the room adjoining Jensen's office and read Jensen's books. He was as quiet as a mouse, for the slightest noise could be heard in the waiting room. The time dragged in the little "hospital," and Elling found it difficult to keep his thoughts away from Ingrid and Stepan and all that was to happen on Thursday night.

He had not yet received any detailed instructions from

Jensen. Those would come only at the last moment, Jensen had said. So far, Elling could only guess what the instructions would be.

Ingrid had no need to guess, but she had to keep her secret to herself. She could not confide in anyone. She went to school at the right time and seemed to be working calmly and studiously in her usual place. No one could have guessed that on Thursday evening she was going to hit someone on the head with a piece of rusty iron piping.

For Stepan, the strain was deathly serious. He knew that he could not live more than a few days longer in this camp. If his illness and the brutal treatment did not kill him, the commandant's pistol would do so. His only chance was his strong desire to live, which must carry him through until Thursday evening.

The person who took it most calmly was Jensen, the man who had organized it all and the only one who knew the whole plan. He did his duty as usual at the station, greeted everyone pleasantly, and joked with those passengers who were going away, whether they were Norwegians or Germans. One moment he was telling the German soldiers a coarse joke; the next he was teasing them by saying that England was sure to win the war.

Yes, Jensen knew how to put on a mask in front of others. He had several helpers in the escape plan, of course, but it was only he himself who knew how it all hung together.

6 — Clear for Flight

Thursday came and went at a snail's pace. It was December now and very cold, and it snowed intermittently the whole day. Late in the evening it stopped, and toward midnight the town lay white and still, well covered up in its winter clothes. Houses, trees, and the mighty mountains roundabout the village breathed only peace and rest.

But sleep was far away from several people that night. They were all fully dressed, ready for action, each in his appointed place, waiting for the same prearranged signals, almost as if they knew that an air raid was coming.

There were to be two different signals: first, a long whistle from the engine as when a scheduled freight train approached the station; then, about ten minutes later, a short, sharp whistle as the same train left the station. The long whistle meant "Clear for action," the short one "Danger over." According to the timetable, the train was due in the station three minutes after midnight.

The telegraph clerk, Jensen, sat in his office at the station, watching the clock on the wall and thinking of his unseen helpers. Now it was up to them to do their jobs cleverly. Not one of the links in the chain must fail, for if it did, it would mean disaster for all. At last the time had come for the final test. Each of them must act independently now.

He thought over his helpers one by one. Would they all stand the test? First of all, there was Elling, who sat ready for action in the room adjoining his office, with a bundle of clothes and a well-filled package of food on his knees. He was sure of Elling. Jensen had had him there for two days and nights instructing him in his job. Elling was well prepared—he would not fail.

Nor would Ingrid, a splendid girl. Everything so far showed how clever and courageous she was. As a matter of fact, Jensen had considered whether he should not arrange for Ingrid to look after Stepan on his flight, as she would have aroused less suspicion than Elling, but in the end Ingrid had been given another task, the first and perhaps the most important of all. She would certainly carry it through if everything else went according to plan. Willie had given his word of honor to help her.

The fourth indispensable cohelper was the electrician on night duty at the power station. He was in a position to cut off the electric current over the whole district whenever he liked, so why not at a definite signal—for example, a long whistle from a train? And he could also turn it on again whenever it suited him—for example, at a short whistle from the same train. This man was now sitting there listening, with nothing else to do. Jensen felt certain that he would not forget his task.

Finally, there were various members of the railway

staff, and Jensen depended on them as he would on his own brothers.

He pulled out a bag of old cigarette stubs from a drawer, pulled off the paper from some of them, collected all the tobacco in his hand, and rolled it into a new cigarette, which he fitted into his holder. He lit it with a steady hand and smoked calmly. The hands of the clock on the wall pointed to three minutes past midnight.

The freight train had not yet been signaled from the station to the north. It was always late these days. It was only a question of how late. He took up the telephone to find out. About half an hour, he was told.

Not so bad! He sighed, reassured. Not such a bad delay as might be expected now that the engines had to be driven on such inferior coal, sometimes even on wood.

7 — The First Signal

Outside the station there were others who could not take things quite so calmly as Jensen. Ingrid had crept away from home a long time ago, as secretly and silently as a thief in the night. Everyone in the house was asleep; no one knew anything about her, not even her own mother, who would never have allowed her to take part in such a dangerous adventure.

She had crept out of bed, put on her ski pants, her boots, and her parka, scarcely daring to breathe. The new snow deadened the sound of her footsteps on the road. As she neared the prisoner-of-war camp, it began to snow again. The white covering on the ground and the trees lightened the night, so she had no need to use her flashlight.

Everything was so dead and still around her that she felt completely alone and almost helpless. If only she had Elling walking beside her! He was thinking of her now, she told herself. He was awake and ready for action, even if she did not know what part he was playing in Jensen's plan.

In any case, it all depended on her whether the others would be able to carry out the plan or not.

She lifted her left arm and felt the right sleeve of the parka carefully, perhaps for the tenth time. Yes, the weapon lay in its right place. She tried to breathe deeply and calmly but felt her heart beating quickly beneath her coat.

She shuddered. Some large dark pines along the road made her suddenly feel like a child who has lost its way in the forest. She felt frightened, almost like crying and calling for her mother. But then she forced herself to think of Stepan and that time when he had cried. Poor, poor Stepan!

Ingrid pushed the tears back angrily. She would save Stepan from that horrible Captain Schnell! She would snatch him away right under the nose of that dressed up Prussian bully! She would show what Norwegian girls were made of! The fury of her thoughts made her increase her speed until she was almost running. She reached her destination well ahead of time and crouched down in the ditch beside the road.

On the other side of the road, about fifty or sixty yards away, was the entrance to the camp, and in the pale light above the entrance she saw a solitary figure. That must be Willie. There he stood in his steel helmet, with his rifle and bare bayonet. He, too, must be prepared for the role he was to play, the role he had promised to play for her sake.

And Stepan—he must not hesitate. He must come immediately! Out of the second barrack door to the left! She hoped he was strong enough to stand upright on his legs.

Now that she thought of it, anything might happen in the last moment to upset the whole plan. Would everything fall into place as soon as the signal went? She wished she could feel absolutely and entirely sure.

She sat on her heels in the snow and listened for the first signal. She was much too early. When the phosphorescent hand of her wristwatch approached midnight, she had been sitting there for about half an hour. Her teeth chattered both from cold and excitement.

Willie was no longer standing still; he was marching up and down in order to keep warm. He stamped hard on the ground, for as a soldier in the occupying army, there was no reason for him to keep quiet.

When the hand of her watch passed twelve o'clock, Ingrid could no longer keep calm. She got up, went over to Willie, and stopped a few yards away from him.

"Willie?" she whispered toward his back.

"Is that you, Ingrid?" the answer came immediately.

"Yes."

"I have been waiting for you."

"I have been here for an eternity." She went right over to him.

"Be careful," he warned. "You had better go and hide yourself again. One never knows what may happen."

"But you're ready, aren't you, Willie?"

"Yes, you may depend on me."

She went back a few steps and found herself a place away from the road but much nearer to the gate this time.

Now she felt calmer; it had helped her to speak to some-one, particularly her nearest "collaborator."

Her wristwatch ticked on, incredibly slowly.

Three minutes past, five minutes past. The snow fell as closely and silently as ever. No sound came from any living creature. There was no sign of the noisy engine they were all waiting for, the engine that was roaring its way toward them through the mountains to the north, the engine that must soon be here and that would give the signal that would help a human being in need.

Ingrid knew that she had to reckon with a delay perhaps of almost an hour, if not more. She had to control her thoughts, cut them off from the excitement of the moment, if possible, dream of something far away. She tried to force herself to do this and at the same time chase away the cold, but it was no easy battle. She felt as if she had been fighting desperately against herself for a whole night when at last the distant sound of rolling wheels against the rails reached her. She started and stood up quickly. She could not mistake that rhythmic thudding and the snorting of the engine. The train must be fairly near; the snow and the mountains had probably deadened the sound farther off.

Now for it! No longer did the countryside sleep silently. An avalanche of sound was set free, and the echo flew from ridge to ridge. It was as if the giants in the mountains had roused themselves to attack the stillness of the night.

41

Ingrid crept across the road and almost as far as the gate. She held the piece of tubing in her right hand and her flashlight in the left. Willie had turned his back and stood there quite calmly. She realized that he would not move from that position now. She went close to the gate and looked in. The camp had stronger lights than those in ordinary houses, and she saw quite plainly that the second barrack door to the left stood ajar.

Then the whistle blew—a long hoarse, dismal howl, a cutting blast like the shriek of a dying monster, a howl that sent shudders through all those standing in the darkness waiting for it. The whistle of a steam engine is never a pretty sound, but this night it seemed incredibly awful, thought Ingrid.

She rushed toward Willie's back with lifted arm. While the echo of the whistle was still tossing to and fro, she saw him throw his rifle away, unlock the gate and drop his keys on the ground, and then hold his helmet up with both hands. He was ready.

Ingrid lifted the tube high above her head, aimed, and brought it down with all her strength in the middle of the steel helmet. With a start she felt her weapon jump out of her hand and fall down in the snow. At that moment the echo died away and the electric lights went out. She caught a glimpse of Willie as he fell on his face and lay quite still. Now she acted quickly and mechanically according to her instructions. She snapped on her flashlight and went through the gate, turning to the left toward bar-

42

rack number two. Stepan had come out shutting the door noiselessly behind him.

"Stepan," she whispered. "Come."

He did not answer, only held out his hand. She took it and pulled him after her out of the gate and down the road.

It was only a few minutes from the camp to the station, but Stepan could not have gotten there without help, not so much because of his illness but because he could scarcely see a yard in front of him in the darkness. Most of the Russian prisoners were as blind as moles in the dark because there was so little fat in their diet that it affected their eyesight.

Ingrid hurried along with Stepan beside her. They heard the train come into the station and stop. They increased their speed as much as Stepan could manage, as if they were trying to catch an express train and not an easy-going freight train.

Ingrid had cherished a secret hope that she might see Elling when they reached the station. She tried to push it aside as it was not important at this moment—at present only Stepan mattered.

They were on a narrow side road, and they entered the station through a gate. Jensen popped up on the other side of the gate. As calmly as if he were helping an ordinary passenger, he took Stepan's arm and pulled him gently away from Ingrid.

Then he leaned toward her and whispered in her ear,

"Good girl, smartly delivered. Hurry off home and go to bed."

Then Ingrid suddenly realized why she was standing there with empty hands.

"Oh, the iron pipe," she whispered to Jensen. "I lost it in the snow!"

Jensen whistled softly. "Well, well never mind," he answered, "but it was a good thing you told me. Right about turn, home."

Ingrid obeyed the order, although she was a little disappointed and went back onto the high road. She comforted herself with the thought that it was best not to know more of the escape plan than was absolutely necessary.

8 — Elling Takes Over

"Now it's your turn," said Jensen to Elling. They were standing in pitch darkness outside the last car, a locked freight car far beyond the end of the platform. Jensen was holding Stepan's arm, and they were waiting for the conductor to come and open the door for them.

"I'm ready," said Elling tensely.

"You know what you've got with you on the journey?"

Elling recited: "Food for two days, ration cards for both of us, clothes for Stepan, matches, a candle, a pair of spectacles, a false beard, and a broken hearing aid."

"Splendid. But you've forgotten the most important."

"Oh, of course—the frontier passes."

"Right. What's Stepan's name?"

"Anders Krooken. Old-age pensioner. I call him Uncle Anders. He is almost completely deaf and never speaks. He only points to his hearing aid and murmurs 'broken' or 'no good.'"

These frontier passes puzzled Elling. How had Jensen managed to get hold of them? Everybody had to have such cards in order to enter the districts bordering on the Swedish frontiers, and the ones that Jensen had given him and

Stepan were exactly like the ordinary legal passes for the Eastern Zone, with numbers, photographs, stamps, and the police signature, all apparently absolutely genuine.

"Good," said Jensen and went on with his instructions. "The first thing you have to do as soon as the train has left the station is to light your candle and ask Stepan to change into the Norwegian civilian clothes as quickly as possible. Then wrap his prisoner's clothes up into a bundle, and when the engine whistles for the next tunnel, a quarter of an hour from here, throw them out through the door on the right. There is a slope there that is so sharp the bundle will roll down and turn into a fine snowball. Understood?"

"Next tunnel. Right door," Elling repeated.

"As a matter of fact, this snow is a tremendous piece of luck. All our traces are fast disappearing."

(Jensen had arranged an extra precaution, which he did not tell Elling. The track watchman was going to keep a lookout for Stepan's clothes the next day when he drove along the track. He was to have paraffin with him to burn the clothes.)

"Tremendous luck," Elling agreed.

Stepan smiled and nodded. He had learned a little Norwegian and understood the word for "luck."

"This freight train divides at Hamar," continued Jensen. "The front cars will be attached to another train to Oslo, and the back cars will go with the same engine to Elverum. Understood?"

"Understood."

"You and Uncle Anders must remain in the carriage

46

and not appear until you have reached Elverum station. This is important. Repeat."

"Not appear before Elverum station," repeated Elling.

"There you will go into the Express Goods Department and greet them from me. Ask for Peter. Any of the boys there will understand who you mean and will direct you. But do not forget to mention my name. Tell Peter that you and your Uncle Anders are to be driven to Stølen immediately. If he asks about money, say that it will come. You will then have a few hours bumping along on bad roads. At Stølen the people will send for the district doctor to see to Stepan."

"Uncle Anders," Elling corrected him.

"Right! The doctor must decide when Uncle Anders is strong enough to undertake the long ski trip. If he can go at once, you will go with him. If not, you will come back here immediately. Now have you got it all in your head?"

"Yes! The Express Goods Department—Peter—Stølen—the district doctor."

"Good, and if you meet a sledge or two on the way, remember the bolder you are, the better."

"The bolder the better," Elling repeated correctly, but his voice was not quite so steady.

"Here comes the conductor. Good-by, both of you. And good luck!"

"Good-by, Jensen."

The conductor had arrived with his bunch of keys. He was as silent as a sphinx and said neither hello nor good-by, nor did he look at anything beyond his keys when he opened the door and pushed the two into the carriage, leaving the door so that it could be opened from the inside. It was only half full of goods, so that the two stowaways, feeling about in the dark, were able to find a box for each to sit on.

Almost at once they heard Jensen's call of "All clear!" followed by a signal from the conductor's whistle and a short blast from the engine—the "Danger over" signal to all the others. Then the train lumbered out of the station.

"Just as slowly and calmly as an ordinary train," mumbled Elling to cheer himself up. Actually he felt more courageous now that they were really off. He had been trembling inside while the train stood still.

Happily he had no time to sit and think over the situation now. He must go on following instructions. He brought out the candle, lit it, and fastened it in its own drippings on the floor. At the same time he explained to Stepan that he must quickly change his clothes. Both Stepan and he could speak German, so they understood each other well.

Stepan looked pale and tired in this light. He was no doubt suffering more pain than he would acknowledge. He began to undress with a grateful smile. His prisoner-of-war clothes were not worth keeping, for they were torn and worn out—a padded Russian uniform jacket without the padding, badly patched trousers, stockings without heels or toes, worn-out boots, underclothes that hung together only by a thread here and there between the holes.

He put on good Norwegian winter clothes, both under-clothes and top clothes (where they came from Elling had

48

not been told). These made Stepan look much better, in fact, quite a new man.

Vaguely Elling saw Stepan transfer a lot of rubbish from his old pockets to the new ones, among it some bits of metal, but he had other things to concentrate on, so that he did not bother to think what they might be. Not until long afterwards did it dawn on him that they were the parts of the secret present to Ingrid and himself. Stepan had not left it behind.

When "Uncle Anders" had put on his beard, spectacles, and hearing apparatus, he was transformed immediately into a really splendid old-age pensioner and grandfather. His appearance tallied exactly with the false identification card. For a moment, the two of them forgot the gravity of the situation, clapped each other on the shoulders, and laughed aloud.

Elling packed Stepan's rags and tatters into the old Russian uniform jacket and tied the jacket sleeves together. Then he took up his place close to the right-hand door, ready to throw them out. Everything went according to Jensen's plans. A few moments later Elling heard the engine whistle, pulled open the door, and slung the bundle of clothes out into the darkness.

Immediately afterwards the train entered the tunnel.

9 — Captain Schnell Joins the Chase

When the engine gave the short blast for "Danger over," there were at least three people in the neighborhood who heaved a sigh of relief.

One was Ingrid, for to her it meant that Stepan had gotten right away from Captain Schnell's clutches. She could sleep calmly now, at any rate for tonight.

The second was the electrician on duty, for now he could put on the electric current again before many people had begun to realize that it was off. It had been off for only a quarter of an hour, so it would be easy for him to plead a small technical fault.

Number three was Willie, the guard, who had continued to lie with his nose in the snow waiting only for the signal before he got up again. The blow from Ingrid's weapon had not hurt him in the least (of course it was not meant that it should), but it had made a pretty good dent in his steel helmet.

As a matter of fact, Willie had been so absorbed in falling to the ground in a natural way that he had not noticed the weapon itself had fallen a yard away from him.

Now he shivered right through his uniform and was glad to get up and tramp warmth back into his body again, but he could not be entirely happy—for the worst part of his job was still to come. He must report the "attack." That would start the alarm and then—

Well, he would act as noiselessly as possible so that Captain Schnell should not be awakened. It had been agreed that he would pretend to be half stunned and therefore confused in his head, so it would be natural enough for him to forget such a small thing as the alarm siren.

The vision of Ingrid's long fair hair and blue eyes had been with him all the time. Only he himself knew how hopelessly and burningly in love with her he was. Only he knew that it was for her sake he had done all this. He was very sorry for Stepan, but his sympathy was not strong enough to make him forsake his duty as a German soldier. But a girl like Ingrid could get him to do anything she wished. Love was too weak a word; he was completely infatuated with her.

When Willie stumbled into the guard room with his dented steel helmet under his arm, there was quite a commotion. The soldier nearest the door woke the officer of the watch and immediately started the siren. It shrieked and howled in its usual ear-splitting way; the searchlight was turned on and, rotating sharply, swept over every corner of the camp, and at the same time the guards rushed out onto the parade ground fully armed. The officer of the watch ordered a man into each of the barracks to see if any of the prisoners had escaped.

While all this was going on, the thing that Willie had most feared happened—Captain Schnell dashed into the camp at top speed. He lived in a villa in the neighborhood that had been requisitioned by the Germans as staff headquarters. He had pulled on his riding breeches, his boots, and his cap and was buttoning up his coat as he ran.

He immediately took command. It was not enough for the soldiers to go through the barracks; he ordered all the prisoners out onto the square in their nightclothes. They were not allowed to put on any shoes but had to stand barefoot in the snow and at attention.

When the commandant discovered that it was Stepan who was missing, he bellowed an order telling the prisoners to stay where they were and in the same position until morning. Anyone who moved was to be shot at sight.

The fact that Captain Schnell did not himself shoot anyone in his fury was no doubt due to the fact—as Willie had foretold—that he was out first and foremost after Stepan. If he could catch him, he could shoot him in triumph on the square with all the other prisoners looking on as "a warning"—as the Germans called that sort of execution.

Willie had to stand at attention while the commandant examined him as to what had happened. But Willie had not much to tell. He had been hit on the head and had fallen down. That was all he could remember of what had happened. Captain Schnell had to content himself with that. As proof, there was the dent in Willie's steel helmet.

He made Willie show him the place where the "attack" had taken place, and in the glare of the searchlight Ingrid's piece of iron tubing was found. The commandant picked it up. At first he could not believe that this was the instrument that had been used. It seemed too simple, almost stupid. He thought that the attacker must have left this weapon behind to mislead the pursuers and put them on the wrong track. But for safety's sake he took the piece of piping with him so that it might be examined with German thoroughness.

Furious and impatient, he tramped around the camp, giving orders and behaving as if he did not wish to lose a minute in the search for this foolhardy prisoner. One of the soldiers had gone to fetch his car, and after a few moments it arrived. Captain Schnell rushed out and took his place in it.

"To the mayor! Quickly!" he barked. The orderly started the car immediately, and it disappeared in a cloud of snow.

The mayor was a young, inexperienced man who had lately been appointed to the position. The old mayor had been dismissed by the Nazis because he was too friendly to the English, and the Germans thought they could not depend on him. This new one had a special cross on the lapel of his coat, showing that he belonged to the Quisling party, was a trusted member of the National Assembly, and collaborated with the Germans. He had already done a few small services for the commandant, like getting sausages and mountain butter for him, and in exchange he had been given tobacco and German brandy. In fact, the two might almost have been called buddies.

Therefore, the mayor was not in the least frightened

when Captain Schnell and his orderly came knocking at his door in the middle of the night. He pulled on some clothes and within five minutes stood ready for anything in his office.

The commandant quickly explained the whole matter.

"Do you know any persons who might keep a Russian in hiding?"

"Well, there're plenty of idiots in the district," answered the mayor.

"Give me their names and addresses," shouted the commandant. "All houses must be searched immediately. Take down the names, orderly."

The orderly took out a pad and pencil, and the mayor dictated. He had grown up in the district and therefore knew all the names and addresses by heart, so the dictation went ahead at a great pace. Then the orderly sat down at the telephone and arranged for patrols to be sent out while the commandant went on talking with the mayor.

"Are there any other places to which he could have fled?" Captain Schnell asked.

"He could have gone into the forest or up into the mountains," said the mayor. "There are plenty of huts up there in which he could take shelter."

"Impossible. The man could scarcely walk. And his helpers, if he had any, could hardly drag him through the snow all that way."

"No, but he might have gotten away in some sort of vehicle."

"North or south, do you think?"

"Probably south and then east. No doubt he has planned to get to Sweden, like so many other fools nowadays."

"Well, we'll put a stop to that!" Captain Schnell banged the table with his fist. "We'll get him tonight!"

"He may have gotten onto the train," remarked the mayor.

"What train?"

"The freight train. The only one that passes here during the night."

"Of course, the freight train!" shouted the commandant. "It must be searched. Where can we do that?"

"Not before Lillehammer. It doesn't stop before that."

"Excellent. Orderly, ring the military police at Lillehammer! Immediately! Tell them to send a patrol to search every car on that train!"

10 — The Train Disaster

Stepan and Elling each sat on a box and shook and jolted down through the Gudbrand Valley. Stepan was the tireder of the two, and after he had had a good share of Elling's food parcel, he curled himself up on his box and fell fast asleep.

Elling also would have liked to sleep, but his tense nerves did not relax so quickly. He only dozed a little, soothed by the sleep-inducing thud of the wheels against the rails.

An hour or more must have passed when he suddenly sat up straight, wide awake. The wheels were not thudding as rhythmically as before. Then came some hard, uneven bumps, which made the car thump quite differently from before. Happily it did not wake Stepan, who was curled up in his corner, sleeping better than he had slept for a long time.

Elling grew more and more nervous. Was something wrong with the wheels? And what would happen if there was? His imagination began to invent stories about derailment, fire, collisions, and every form of train disaster he could think of.

Suddenly he saw a light flash across the chink in the door. He crept up and looked out. A rain of sparks flew up from one of the wheels. So there really was something seriously wrong after all! This sort of thing might lead to a fire or anything else you might like to think of.

"The whole plan of flight is spoiled," he thought despondently. They could not possibly get away in time after such a misfortune, for Captain Schnell would be sure to start the chase early next morning. They would both be caught in the German network.

He went back to his box and brooded. Should he wake Stepan? No, that would not help at all. Besides, this sleep was probably doing Stepan a world of good.

The rain of sparks outside had now died down, and it seemed as if the bumping was less. Elling began to hope for the best.

Then it all began again. The sparks and the bumping and the shaking grew dangerously violent. Then they diminished and after an interval began again. It went on like this for a long time.

At first Elling felt shaken and exhausted by all this; then he grew more and more apathetic, and at last fatigue gained the upper hand. He fell into a restless doze, full of fantasies about fights with Germans, imprisonment, and torture.

Both he and Stepan woke when the thumping and the shaking came to a sudden stop. The train was standing still. Everything was so calm and quiet around them that Elling did not wish to risk drawing attention to them by lighting his candle. They heard the hissing of the steam in the engine far away in front.

Stepan whispered in the dark, "Where are we now, Elling?"

"Don't know. I've been asleep."

"Why are we standing still?"

"I think there is something wrong with one of the wheels underneath us here."

Then they heard voices approaching and listened silently.

"They're talking Norwegian," whispered Elling.

"Good." Stepan sighed.

The voices outside stopped, and they heard steps coming nearer. They sat quietly without moving, waiting.

A pale blue light came in through the crack in the door, and then it was opened from outside.

The conductor's voice shouted gaily, "Last stop before Lillehammer! A long wait! No restaurant!"

It was the conductor who had locked them in some hours earlier. He was not so silent now, perhaps because now he alone had the responsibility for them.

"What is the matter?" asked Elling nervously. "Can't we go any farther?"

"A damaged wheel," answered the conductor shortly. "We must leave the car here. It's only by pure luck that we got it as far as this."

"And—and you'll leave us, too?"

"Yes, that's just the question. It's the only closed freight car in the whole train. You'll be turned into icicles if you go into one of the open flat cars. We could take you with us in the brake car, but the head conductor doesn't want to. He's certain that something will happen if we do. He himself is already under suspicion with the Germans, you see, because his son has gotten away to England and for several other things as well. If there's any trouble now, he is afraid that the whole family will be sent to a concentration camp."

Elling swallowed and tried to make his voice as grown-up as possible.

"I understand. We must find another way out."

"We have plenty of time. This train has to reload in Lillehammer for two hours before it goes on. In the meantime, they will send a truck up to get the freight out of this car and to check the damage. You can come on with the truck, and I'll find you a freight car with undamaged wheels to take you to Hamar."

"Thanks a lot, conductor."

"And if the truck does not come, the rail lineman will find transport for you. I'll wake him now. He'll be getting up soon, anyhow. Then you can get something warm into your bodies. You'll like that, won't you?"

"Yes—sure!" Elling visualized a blazing fire with crackling logs, and no one could have offered him anything better at that moment. Both he and Stepan felt stiff and cold after their journey.

"Come along with you! He lives just over there."

The conductor went in front of them, lighting their way with his torch across the rails of an unknown station. They went on along the lines to a low little house. The conductor rolled a snowball and threw it at the window.

A few minutes later they were sitting in front of just the fire that Elling had imagined and felt the warmth from the logs streaming through their frozen bodies. The little gray-haired lineman and his round, smiling wife bustled about, looking after them as if they had been their own sick children. Their faces were full of curiosity, but they asked no unnecessary questions—for instance, where these nocturnal freight-train passengers had come from and where they were going. They realized what was at stake, that this was someone fleeing from the Germans who needed help. In such a case, no questions were asked; one only helped.

Elling could tell nothing, and Stepan only smiled and pointed to his hearing aid, whispering, "Broken, no good."

The lineman's wife brought out things that could be obtained only on the black market, sausages, goats' milk cheese, home-baked bread, and even a few beans of real coffee that she had been keeping for Christmas.

The conductor went back to his duties. They heard the useless carriage being shunted onto another track, and then the train continued on its way. They sat enjoying the glorious warmth, both the warmth from the fire and also the heartfelt warmth of these two dear old people. A clock ticked calmly away in a corner, adding to their relaxed condition as time passed.

Then the service telephone on the wall rang. The lineman rose and picked up the receiver. There followed quite a short conversation. The lineman stood and listened for a few seconds; then he said, "Yes," and put back the receiver.

The other three saw that he had turned pale and that his hand was shaking a little. He remained by the telephone as if he were thinking deeply.

"Was that from Lillehammer?" asked his wife. "You look so serious!"

"Yes, it was not pleasant news. The Germans have closed the station. A patrol from the military police is searching the freight train at this moment, every inch of it, in fact. They are sending the repair truck along immediately to shift the damaged carriage that has been left behind here. It also will have German guards on it."

It was Elling's turn to grow pale.

"So they are suspicious already," he said in a low voice. "How in the world . . ."

"This is no time to speculate," the lineman broke in. "If you want to save your skins, you must get away from here—and quickly too!"

"But Uncle Anders is ill—he can't walk far. Is there anything in which we can drive?"

"Nothing but the handcar. We can use that for a short distance. It is just about time for my inspection of the line, anyhow."

Cold shivers went down Elling's back. Then he remembered Jensen's words: "The bolder the better!" Now he would prove how true they were. The chance had come sooner than anyone had dreamed it would. Here was a chance to trick the Germans if he were bold enough. In clear daylight, too, for it was no longer dark. Dawn was lighting the sky outside the windows.

"All right," he said to the lineman. "We'll meet the repair truck about halfway to Lillehammer, I suppose?"

"Yes, probably."

"Then Uncle Anders and I will jump off and hide ourselves until it has gone on, and then we'll jump on the handcar again and continue!"

The lineman nodded. "I had thought of something like that myself, but God only knows where you will go if I can take you no farther."

"It will work out all right," said Elling, and he tried to appear calm and sure of himself. "I'll hide Uncle Anders somewhere and go out and look for help. I can go wherever I like; no one suspects me."

"That's all right, as long as you have luck with you! Come on, let's go at once. I wonder if there is anything suspicious over there in the freight car."

"I'll go and have a look."

Elling ran off and inspected their night's lodging while the lineman prepared the handcar. Elling found nothing in the freight car that could in any way betray them except candle grease on the floor. He kicked away the worst of it and moved a heavy box over the rest.

When he got back, the handcar was ready to start. The lineman's wife came out with two blankets for the passengers and wrapped them up in a motherly way. She had also prepared a package of food for each of them and pushed them both down into Stepan's pockets. He smiled gratefully and stammered a thank-you. Then the lineman set off slowly while his wife waved and smiled.

The two passengers shielded their eyes with their hands and kept a lookout as they rode along. The lineman laughed at them and said they need not take it quite so seriously.

"I'll be the one to discover the repair truck first," he asserted.

"Why?" asked Elling.

"With my ears—long before my eyes catch a glimpse of it."

"Oh, I see—"

But Elling continued to stare along the track because, as he thought, one never knows.

The lineman was right. As they emerged from a cutting in the mountain, he suddenly stopped the handcar and told them to take their blankets and go and hide themselves. Neither Stepan nor Elling had noticed anything at all.

They found some close-growing pine bushes for a hiding place, and they carefully brushed away their footprints and smoothed the snow with one of the blankets. The lineman went on a little farther. Then he stopped again and lifted the handcar off the rails. He was quite right. A strange-looking vehicle came around a curve a little farther on. Elling and Stepan huddled down into the snow. From here they could both see and hear what went on.

The repair truck braked hard close to the handcar. A head in a German steel helmet came out of the driver's cabin and a voice shouted to the lineman in a kind of German-Norwegian.

"You seen a man about here?"

"Nope," answered the lineman shortly.

"Sure?"

"Yes."

"You see no one—on the whole line?"

"Nope."

"Nor at the station?"

"Nope!"

The steel helmet was drawn back into the driver's cabin, and the repair truck went on. It had gained its top speed as it passed the two behind the bushes and disappeared into the cutting.

They came out of hiding and followed the railway line to the handcar.

"You got through that fine," said Elling admiringly.

"I'm pretty good at German," answered the lineman and spat out a long line of snuff into the snow. "Get up, both of you, and we'll get on."

They rode on in peace and without speaking for several miles, until they neared the suburbs of Lillehammer. Below them, on their right, lay the river, white and covered with ice along its edges. The town itself was not far away, and Elling felt cold shivers down his back again, for he knew that a German patrol was there awaiting them.

The lineman looked around carefully and then stopped the handcar for the last time. They were close to a path used for shifting timber.

"From here you can get down quite easily to the river and other places," he explained. "Over in that field you can see some timber drivers, and I think it would be worth your while to speak to them. I cannot think of any better advice to give you at the moment."

Elling and Stepan got off the car, leaving the blankets behind them. The lineman folded them up and put them in his toolbox.

"Thank you for lending them to us," said Elling heavily. He had a big lump in his throat and felt anything but bold now that they were going to be left entirely alone. "And thanks a million for the ride, lineman."

"Th-thank you," Stepan added.

The lineman looked away from them and busied himself spitting snuff.

"Nothing to thank me for," he said in a low voice. "Best of luck."

When the alarm went off in the prison camp, it was heard as clearly at the station as any signal from an incoming train, but it was much weaker in the house where Ingrid lived. Ingrid pulled the blanket over her head as she did not want to hear anything more. She had had enough for one night, she thought.

Jensen, however, joined in with a gay little whistle, which he kept going as long as the alarm lasted. He had been prepared for this possibility and did not allow himself to be disturbed. The worst possible thing anyone could do in a dangerous situation, Jensen knew, was to lose his self-control or his sense of humor. A man should never stop whistling and singing if he had a dangerous job to do, whether it was in war or in peace.

He did his usual round quite calmly, put out all the lights, locked up the waiting room and the office. The station would be dark for the rest of the night.

He whistled without stopping while he did all this and meanwhile thought up a story to tell—a story about the iron piping. They would no doubt soon find out that it came from the station. He had been a little careless there.

He could not blame Ingrid for having lost the weapon at the critical moment. That sort of thing can happen to anyone. She had carried out the job brilliantly for a girl of sixteen; yes, she was quite outstanding. They would not have been able to get the escape plan going without her.

Jensen went into his room and threw himself down on the bed to think further. It was not long before he began to chuckle and hum to himself. He had thought of something, a story that might be both amusing and useful. Now let them come.

He put on his pajamas, turned out the light, and fell asleep with the best conscience in the world.

He only half woke up when Captain Schnell's men brought their motorcycles right onto the station platform. He was only half awake when they poked around the station and finally rang the stationmaster's bell on the second floor of the building. He felt rather maliciously pleased when he heard that his superior had to get up and give them all the keys.

The soldiers ransacked everything from the luggage office to the cloakroom, and finally they also knocked on Jensen's door. He did not get up but yawned loudly from his bed. They spoke to him politely as they knew him from the freight department and had often enjoyed his jokes and good humor. When he assured them that there were lots of Russian prisoners hidden beneath his bed, they laughed loudly and disappeared with a hearty *"Wieder-schau'n!"* and *"Schlafen Sie wohl!"*

It was not until late the next morning that the German

staff car arrived. Jensen had had a good sleep, had eaten his usual war breakfast for bachelors (a cup of ersatz coffee, black bread covered with a thin layer of margarine, and cod caviar) when he heard the commandant's voice out in the office. It sounded cross from lack of sleep, and he barked more sharply than usual.

The stationmaster was on duty that morning, so he was interrogated first. After that the porter. Then Jensen was called into the office.

There sat Captain Schnell with the piece of iron tubing in his hand, and on a chair a little farther away sat his orderly. Between them there was another chair, and Jensen was told to sit down.

The commandant tried to impale him with a glance.

"Have you seen this piece of iron before?" he asked and pushed it right under the nose of the suspected one.

"Well-ll—that's possible," answered Jensen, wrinkling his forehead and looking as if he were thinking very deeply.

"It's possible, did you say? Perhaps you have used it?"

Jensen shook his head.

"It looks as if it has belonged to some sort of brake."

"Right! But it has been used for something quite different. For example, it might be used for hitting people over the head, mightn't it?" said the commandant, giving Jensen a light blow on his forehead with the weapon.

"Thank you," answered Jensen drily.

Captain Schnell bent forward toward him.

68

"Perhaps, for example, you yourself, Mr. Jensen, have used this piece of iron as a weapon!"

Jensen started back in his chair.

"I can assure you, Herr Commandant, that I have never hit anybody on the head with a piece of iron tubing."

"Not even allowed it to fall on a German steel helmet?"

"Not in this world, Herr Commandant!"

"Well, we'll soon find that out, my good man. You told my advance patrol that you sent off the freight train last night without noticing anything suspicious. Is that right?"

"That's right."

"Absolutely nothing suspicious? No possibility for any-one to sneak on board the train?"

"No one could have caught me out, Herr Commandant. There was not a suspicious person to be seen anywhere." (Elling and Uncle Anders were certainly not suspicious characters, Herr Commandant, he added internally.)

"Well, well, back to this piece of iron. You think that you recognize it?"

Once more Jensen wrinkled his forehead and looked as if he were seriously trying to think before he answered.

"Yes, now I remember it. Yes, I really think I do."

"Tell me! At once! Immediately!"

"Well, I think that piece of iron tubing lay on a heap of scrap iron that we had at the station some time ago. The heap lay behind the storehouse at the farthest end."

"What happened to it? Tell me quickly!"

"Someone came and bought it."

"When?"

"Quite a few months ago, I think."

"Who bought it? You *must* remember."

"A chap we call the junkman."

"Who is that?"

"He's not a real junk merchant; he only bought up that little lot on spec."

"What is he called? Where does he live?"

"Well-ll, I cannot remember the name exactly," replied Jensen, bluffing, "for I am not really from this district. But I know the house."

"Show it to me immediately!"

The commandant stood up. The orderly jumped up and opened the door for him. All three went quickly out onto the platform.

Jensen pointed the way to a small farm lying to the north of the district. They immediately got into the staff car and drove off.

Their informant remained on the platform chuckling. He would have liked to see Captain Schnell's face when he found out who the "junk merchant" was, also the face of the "junk merchant." Up there in that little farm the commandant would find one of the most ardent Nazi families in the district, with a large crooked cross over the entrance.

But the man who had bought the scrap iron lived there no longer. He had moved to a better house. A few months ago he had been given a new job—as mayor.

12 — Timber Hauling

Stepan leaned on Elling's shoulder as they struggled down the slippery slope toward the river. He leaned heavily, for he was very ill and his emaciated body extremely weak. But his cheerfulness overcame all difficulties. He smiled broadly every time Elling looked at him and joked about his own weakness in an amusing mixture of German, Norwegian, and Russian. Elling was never obliged to cheer him up; it was the other way around, for Stepan always gave courage to Elling when the situation was at its blackest.

They reached the banks of the river. The snow-covered ice was firm for about three feet from the bank, but after that there was open water. About a hundred yards from where they stood a timber driver was loading his sled. He was alone.

Stepan found a stump of a tree on which he could sit, well hidden from inquisitive eyes.

"I'll sit here while you go and speak to the driver," he suggested.

"All right," said Elling, "but what if he is a Nazi!"

"I don't suppose there are very many Nazi timber drivers in Norway." Stepan smiled encouragingly.

71

"We shall see." Elling lifted his hand to his cap in a friendly salute to "Uncle Anders" and went to find out.

The timber driver was a middle-aged man with a large, coarse face and tufts of reddish brown hair sticking out from under his ski cap. He looked at the boy who was approaching him with a little surprise but went on with his loading.

"Good morning," said Elling tentatively. "You are loading timber."

"True enough," answered the driver, wiping his nose with the back of his glove. "Of course I'm loading timber —anyone could see that."

"Is there a lot of timber to be driven away this winter?" said Elling.

"Well, so far we've had enough work to keep us going."

"It's been good hauling weather lately?"

"Not too bad for driving and the cold not too bad, either. But it's a bit heavy now with all this new snow."

"Do you need any help?"

The man smiled, and a number of wrinkles appeared on his broad face.

"Oh, I get on all right by myself, but who are you when it comes to that? You're not from this district; I can hear that by your accent."

"No, I'm traveling."

The question had rather upset Elling, and he felt that he must produce some plausible story before the man became too curious.

"It's awful with this war that will never come to an end, it seems," he added.

"Oh, it can't last forever," answered the man in a matter-of-fact voice.

"How long do you think?"

"Not so easy to say, but soon there'll be no food, so it can't go on for more than another winter, I guess."

Hm, this did not tell him much, thought Elling. Which side is he on? Perhaps I must ask him outright after all.

"At any rate, things are beginning to go better on the Eastern Front," said he, waiting tensely for the answer.

"Perhaps so," said the driver.

"The Germans are retiring everywhere."

"It doesn't look like that from the papers."

Goodness, could it be that he read only the ordinary papers that were so sure of victory for the Germans? Did he never hear the "real" news, the news that all good Norwegians knew even though such news was spread about in a secret manner.

"Surely you don't believe the papers," said Elling boldly.

The man looked at him and kept his eyes fixed on him for a moment.

"Oh no," he answered at last. "I don't believe any of the nonsense they tell us in the papers, but I wondered what sort of chap you were. You might be one of those Nazi youths for all I know."

Elling was obliged to laugh.

"That is just what I thought about you. But after all, we are both good Norwegians, aren't we?"

"Most of us are," said the driver. "In the little place I come from, there is only one who is on the wrong side, out of the three hundred who live there, and he is anyhow not very dangerous."

"No, there are not many who are dangerous. But one can never be too careful."

The man scratched his neck and gazed at Elling in a surprised way again.

"So you have to be careful, have you?"

"Yes, you understand . . ." Elling hesitated. "Where are you taking that load?"

"A mile to the south. Why are you asking?"

"Well I . . . I can't very well tell you everything. I have a sick man with me whom the Germans are after, Uncle Anders. He is sitting on a stump of a tree over there. He can't walk very well, so he has to be driven. But the Germans have surrounded the station at Lillehammer and the main road, too."

The timber driver slowly pulled off one of his gloves and blew his nose with it. Then he took a couple of steps toward his horse, which was standing with its nose in a bag of hay hanging from its neck. He stroked its mane and patted its forehead.

"Well, well, Bronna," he said. "Do you think we can manage to carry a sick man as well as this load, eh?"

Bronna snorted good-naturedly into his nose bag and went on eating.

"That's all right," said the driver. "Bronna has nothing against it, as you hear. Where in the world are you thinking of taking a sick man in this neighborhood?"

"We've got to get to Elverum by some means or other."

"To Elverum, yes. I understand. Bronna and I can't help you on very far. Are you in a hurry?"

"I don't really know. We shall just have to take as much time as we can get."

"Then I think you had better come with me first of all and get a little food into your bodies, and a little warmth, too," he added.

"Yes, thank you, but—perhaps it's best that as few people as possible should see us."

"Keep calm; that's all right. While I'm hauling timber, I live quite alone in a little hut. My family live farther up the valley. Help me with this last tree trunk and then I've finished."

Elling took a good grasp of the tree, they lifted it into place, and the man said "gee-up" to Bronna. Stepan smiled into his beard more broadly than ever and thanked them many, many times when they came and fetched him.

The little gray hut lay a short way up from the banks of the river and a little south of the village itself. The driver drove his sled along roundabout ways so as to avoid the risk of meeting Germans or other inquisitive people.

The driver—his name was Lars—lit a wood fire in his stove and said that now they'd better eat an early dinner with him. As a forest laborer, he was allowed an extra ration of meat, and he shared it with them.

Although he was not desperately hungry, Elling was overcome by greediness when the fat meat frizzled in the pan and its delicious smell filled the little room. He could not remember having any meat at home since last Christmas.

But "Uncle Anders" shook his head and pointed mournfully to his shrunken stomach. He would eat only potatoes. Meat was too strong a diet for anyone who had lived on thin cabbage soup for as long as he had.

But his longing for meat was almost more than he could bear, and the other two persuaded him to try a tiny bit. Five minutes later he had to go outside, where he was violently sick. Then Lars found some dried fish for him, which he was able to digest more easily.

For a long time Lars sat there eating without saying a word. Elling watched him, hoping that maybe he was thinking up a plan and did not want to be disturbed.

Stepan was silent as he usually was in foreign company. He chewed his dried fish absent-mindedly but was alert to what went on for all that. Lars finished eating and then fished his pipe out of his pocket. It was old and shabby, and the mouthpiece was mended with tar paper. He filled it with something looking more like pocket dust than tobacco and lit it.

After a few long puffs his face grew calmer, and it looked as if he had made some sort of decision. He took his pipe out of his mouth, cleared his throat once or twice, and then said calmly and thoughtfully, "When there is disaster and misery in the land, we must all help each other as best we can."

"Yes!" answered Elling eagerly.

76

"One's own job is perhaps not always the most important."

"No! Nor school either."

Lars put his pipe back into his mouth and smoked for a few moments before he went on.

"I have kinfolk and friends along the whole of the river. Bronna might perhaps be willing to take a little trip to Hamar."

Elling's face shone. "To Hamar! From there it would not be very far over to Elverum, and then we would be almost there!" How he was going to evade the Germans the whole way he could not even imagine. "That would be great," Elling continued, "if you could manage it."

"But it is not done in a day. From here to Hamar is at least thirty-five miles. Also, we won't be able to drive along the main road, and Bronna is not a fast-moving horse."

"That doesn't matter. As long as we keep away from railway and motor traffic."

"We can drive along the ice edge here for a bit of the way and then along byways."

"Fine!"

Lars stood up. "Well then, we had better be going. I've no other sled, so we must just use the log one and manage as best we can."

"But what about your load?"

"That can wait till I come back from Hamar. Come along and we'll get going."

13 — Drama

They had driven for several hours by daylight and almost as long in the dark when Lars swung the sled up a farm track in the direction of a speck of light visible through the trees.

Bronna had trotted along mile after mile in a firm, even rhythm, the landscape stretching broadly and gently around them beneath the soft new snow, seeming as untouched and peaceful as if it had never been trampled by the boots of soldiers.

But both Elling and Lars knew better. Just over there on the highway behind those mountaintops, the war had passed and had left nature with its wounds and unhappy memories. Here German commanders and their armored cars had driven about everywhere over the Norwegian countryside, frightening the peaceful inhabitants. These gray vehicles still ruled the main road, but perhaps all that might soon come to an end. At last there seemed a glimmer of hope.

They had met one or two other people in sleds on the way but had not stopped or spoken with anyone. They had also seen Germans here and there, but happily they seemed engaged with other things than looking for runaway prisoners. Everything had gone so calmly and in such an ordinary way that Elling began to ask himself whether the lineman's good-by wishes were not about to be fulfilled.

Lars steered Bronna through an open gate into a little yard. Everything was in darkness, but the horse found his own way to a door in the cattle shed. There he stood still, neighing. No doubt he had followed the scent and now felt glad to think he would soon be in a warm stable.

Loud voices and laughter were heard from inside the house. Lars got down off the sled and began loosing Bronna. Then he turned to his passengers. "You wait out here," he said. "I'll go in and explain everything to them. Louisa, my sister, lives here with my brother-in-law, Bergulv."

First of all he opened the door of the cattle shed, and Bronna went in whinnying. Another horse gave an answering neigh.

Then Lars strode across the dark farmyard and went into the house. Again they heard loud, cheerful voices. Obviously the guest was warmly welcome. Several voices shouted in chorus, "Skål!"

The two on the sled listened tensely.

"Did you hear—they said 'Skål'?" whispered Stepan. "Skål" was one of the first words he had learned in Norwegian.

"Yes, it sounds as if they are enjoying themselves in there," whispered Elling. "I only hope they won't forget us."

But that they certainly did not.

A few minutes later the outer door opened, and four heavy figures strode out into the yard. One of them was swinging a lantern, which was scarcely blacked out at all.

"Welcome to the farm!" shouted the man with the lantern in such a loud voice that he might have been inviting the whole district. "Come in and have a cup of coffee!"

The other three took hold of Stepan, lifted him high off the sled as if he had been a sack of hay, but at the same time handling him gently and with great care. Elling was pushed in just behind the man with the lantern, who was obviously the farmer himself.

They entered a large country kitchen with a long table down the center and rose-patterned cupboards along the walls. On the table were six half-full cups of coffee, a dish of margarine, and a leg of mutton.

A thin but kindly farmer's wife, her head tied in a scarf, greeted them heartily. She was Louisa, Lars's sister.

"You must really excuse us," she said. "It's my husband Bergulv's birthday today, and he insisted on celebrating it in the kitchen, the rascal."

She fetched cups and poured out coffee for the guests.

"It's only ersatz coffee, so you can have a little too," she said to Elling, and he nodded. "Come on, both of you, eat as much as you can manage—today there is no rationing here."

Bergulv went over to a cupboard in the corner and brought out a bottle.

"And here's some brandy." He chuckled and then added, "It's good for travelers coming from far away. How much would you like?"

Elling did not dare take any and Stepan only a mouth-ful.

"No, no," said Bergulv, "it's not everyone who can take spirits as we potato farmers from Hedmarken do. Skål, everybody! Welcome to my birthday party!"

They all responded to the cry of "Skål" with their coffee cups. Then one of the men began to sing a patriotic song, and he was followed by Louisa and then by all the others, one after another. The choir was strong and sincere, even if not very beautiful.

After this song Lars suggested "Sons of Norway," which was sung more loudly than ever. Then, one after the other, they suggested songs from the old free country, which was free no longer.

All the suggestions were applauded and all were sung in turn. The brandy was passed from one to the other, and the singing grew louder and louder so that Bergulv could hardly complain that his birthday atmosphere was not cheerful enough. Louisa tried to make them eat now and again so that they did not drink more than was good for them.

When they had sung all the Norwegian songs and ditties they could think of, the host suddenly remembered that they had forgotten to sing for the deaf guest. Wasn't his name Anders Krooken? "Let's have a song for old Krooken!" Bergulv winked when he said it. He had, no doubt, his suspicions as to what kind of guest it was, and this fact became quite evident from the song he chose. He rose, threw out his arms toward Stepan, and began to sing "The Volga Boatsong" in his tremendous voice. The whole company joined in with all their might and main. The old Russian folk song echoed from the kitchen walls and rose like a clap of thunder through the chimney and out into the winter's night.

"Volga, Volga, Mother Volga!"

Then—just at that very moment—there came a thunderous knock on the outer door. They also heard a few angry kicks on the panel of the door.

The song stopped suddenly; the cheerful faces stiffened. All looked at each other and at Stepan, pale and silent. When anyone knocks at a door that way, he is not a friend.

A loud command was heard from outside—in German. Like a shadow Bergulv was across the floor and out onto the porch.

"Down into the cellar," he whispered to his wife in passing.

Louisa had no doubt as to what it all meant. As Bergulv shut the door behind him, she saw the glint of two German helmets out there.

Like lightning she opened the trap door to the cellar. Two of the men took hold of Stepan and helped him down in a moment. The trap door was shut again, and they put the largest chair over it. It was an action born of desperation, but they had nowhere else to hide him in a hurry.

From the porch they heard a stream of German words that could not be distinguished one from the other, and the voices were not exactly friendly. But there was nothing to be done except wait until the Germans came tramping in with loaded pistols and searched the house from top to bottom for the fugitive. Elling felt his heart beating, and his forehead and hands were bathed in sweat. The excitement outside quieted down by degrees. The German voices grew less noisy. Suddenly they heard Bergulv's voice. Evidently he was trying to explain something. But the only word they could hear was "birthday," which he repeated several times. The Germans mumbled something in answer; then one of them said loudly and clearly, *"Nah, Geburtstag!"*

Then followed one or two indistinct sentences, and the voices came nearer. Bergulv said something just outside the door, and they heard heavy footsteps approaching the kitchen. The tenseness around the long table was almost unbearable. Everybody sat absolutely still.

Then the door flew open and Bergulv came in, and just behind him in the doorway stood two uniformed Germans. A gasp of surprise went through the company when Bergulv shouted, "Wife! Mix two extra strong cups of coffee and brandy immediately!"

Louisa could scarcely believe her own ears, but she did what she was told without turning a hair. The Germans' drinks were mixed in record time and, in addition, made extra strong.

Bergulv handed them the cups, lifted his own cup, and shouted, "Skål, comrades!"

The two German soldiers stood at attention and answered "Skål" and "Happy Birthday!" They each took a deep gulp and wrinkled their noses when they realized how strong it was.

"Skål!" shouted Bergulv again and signed to the others

that they should drink with the Germans. All lifted their cups, and the soldiers had to "skål" again, although they drank rather more carefully this time.

"Sit down!" cried Bergulv. "Have a slice of mutton with your drink!" The Germans smiled and thanked him but said they must be getting on.

"Then sing us a song before you go!" said Bergulv, and without waiting for an answer he himself began singing a Christmas carol. The two soldiers joined in in German, the second one singing very charming "seconds." Soon the whole company was singing in peaceful unison. Stepan was given a strange entertainment down in his black hiding place.

After the song the Germans thanked them again and left. Bergulv went out with them to make sure that they did actually march out of the gate.

When he came back into the kitchen, they all sat and stared at him. Lars was the first to pull himself together.

"Listen, Bergulv," he said, "how on earth did you manage it?"

Bergulv laughed.

"Wait a moment and we'll pull the old man up from the cellar."

They opened the trap door, and a rather bewildered "Uncle Anders" was hauled up. Elling explained to him quickly that the danger was over.

Louisa looked questioningly at her husband. "Well, tell us now, Bergulv!" she begged.

"It was easy enough," he said with a teasing gleam in

his eye. "I said that I was the Prime Minister's brother, so that they better keep away from my house."

"Nonsense!"

"Then I said I had an old blunderbuss in my cellar of which they should have a taste if they dared to come over the threshold. They said 'excuse us' immediately."

"Nonsense! Now tell us the truth, for goodness' sake!"

"Yes, Bergulv, now you're going a little too far with us!" said one of the others.

Most of the members of the company were still a little pale. The shock had made them feel disinclined for jokes.

Bergulv chuckled.

"Well, well, to tell you the truth, those two comrades of ours were not looking for what we thought. They were out checking the blackout, and they had seen a little light and came to investigate. Can you imagine how that can have happened?"

"There isn't a chink in the blackout curtains here in the farmhouse," declared Louisa decidedly.

"No. It was I who had left the stable lantern out on the doorstep," said Bergulv, laughing loudly. They all sank back relieved in their chairs. Elling explained what had happened to Stepan and saw a look of relief spread over his face behind his beard.

"What nonsense!" said Louisa to her husband. "You invite the devil himself to come to the farm. You might well have found yourself in prison for this."

"Don't forget whose birthday it is today," said Bergulv calmly.

"No, I suppose we must blame the drink."

"Skål!"

Coffee cups were swung in the air again. But there was not the same lightheartedness as before. No one thought of singing any more. No one felt inclined to shout.

A man yawned long and loudly, and it infected the others. They remembered that they must be up early tomorrow for a new working day.

Not long afterwards the birthday feast came to an end. Bergulv's friends from the neighboring farms went home, and Louisa made up beds on the floor for the three travelers.

14 — The Mayor Is Angry

That evening Jensen had yet another visitor—the mayor. This young man, who had been newly appointed to this responsible post, looked angry and upset. It was obvious he had not come to pay the station staff a friendly visit. But Jensen was ready for him. He had teased this young man before he became mayor and felt inclined to tease him again.

"Good day, good day, your worship!" he greeted the mayor gaily. "How lovely everything looks with this new snow, don't you think so?"

"Oh, stop your nonsensical talk," shouted the mayor, "you liar!"

"That isn't a very pleasant remark to make," said Jensen, smiling.

"You've tried to throw suspicion on me!"

"You don't say!"

"It was I who bought all that wretched iron tubing, was it?"

"No, indeed, I only told your friend the commandant who it was who used to buy scrap iron roundabout here."

That remark did not tend to made the mayor any better-tempered.

"I've never been a scrap iron merchant!" he shouted. "And mind what you say or I'll go and tell the commandant one or two little things I know about you!"

Jensen stood calmly behind the counter. He put a cigarette stub into his cigarette holder and lit it.

"For example?" he asked coldly.

"For example, that that cigarette holder with which you are smoking was made by a certain Russian prisoner!"

"Indeed?"

"Made specially for a certain telegraph clerk, Jensen, by his friend, a Russian prisoner named Stepan who has now escaped."

"Not bad! Our good mayor is beginning to be quite intelligent! And then?"

"Well, this is not the only thing that a mayor knows. I follow closely everything that happens in this district, you see, even if you don't think so. I know, among other things, about people who listen to forbidden radio programs and spread the news from London. And on a special type of paper, too."

"On writing paper headed with the name of Jensen perhaps?"

"I didn't say so. But don't think that any paper is circulated here in the district that does not sooner or later find its way to the mayor's office!"

"Thanks for the information. I'll tell the head of distribution to take the news straight to your office in the future."

"Don't take that superior tone, Jensen. It may get you into trouble!"

But Jensen paid no attention to warnings. Slowly and carefully he knocked the last little bit of cigarette stub out of his holder into the ash tray and bent over the counter toward his enemy.

"Now listen, mayor," he said in an affected, confidential tone of voice. "You know too little. You don't even know that I have a secret printing press in the cellar that prints the "forbidden" news. Also, I have a hundred kilos of dynamite under my bed with which to blow up the railway line when the English invade us. Every evening I talk to King Haakon and Winston Churchill on the short wave, and they have promised that it will not be long before . . ."

"Don't you dare make fun of me!" the mayor interrupted angrily.

"All right, but you go and tell your German chiefs what you think you know, and then I will tell you what that sort of thing is called in good Norwegian and what the punishment for it will be. It's called treachery."

"I am no informer!"

"You may soon become one. The worst of them have a little coffin sent by post. Next time they lie in a large coffin themselves."

"I have told you I am no informer!" The mayor did not feel at all comfortable now. He stood there twisting and turning.

"It doesn't matter in the least what you consider yourself; it's others who decide what you are to be called.

89

Those glib National Socialists are not as safe in their positions nowadays as they were. It is beginning to be quite the thing to get rid of them, as you no doubt know."

Jensen was now doing his best to frighten the mayor so that he would stop telling tales. His tactics were working.

But the mayor did not want to show openly that he was frightened of the Underground.

"You bloodthirsty people ought to think again," he said scornfully. "The Germans are going to shoot ten Norwegians for anyone who is liquidated."

"Yes, if the murdered man is a German—but not a Norwegian!"

"You have no guarantee for that. You wait; you may be unpleasantly surprised."

"Oh no, Mr. Mayor, it is probably you who will have that surprise, not me. Or do you think that Germany is not going to win?"

"Of course they are! They are pushing forward on all fronts."

"On the propaganda posters, yes. But they are practically defeated in Africa, and these days great things are happening in Stalingrad."

"Stalingrad has fallen. The Germans took the town six weeks ago."

"In Goebbels' propaganda report—yes. But no, old man, Stalingrad is the beginning of the end for the Germans, for when the Russians start their offensive in the winter, it will be a different story—just as it was with Napoleon and Charles XII."

"Ha, ha, English propaganda! Fabricated by Churchill, the whisky king."

"You'll soon find that he's good for much more than whisky drinking."

"And smoking superior cigars! He and King Haakon sit together chatting every evening over there in London. They smoke rather better stuff than the odds and ends that you put in your cigarette holder!"

"You can tell that to the King when he comes home to Norway. Then he will settle his account with various lackeys and subservient mayors!"

"Ha, ha, the King can invent stories about that day, but he'll never be king again if he lives to be a hundred!"

"Quite unnecessary for that—he *is* our King now. But I am not so sure that he will wish to have all types as subjects when he comes back."

"You are as loudspoken as ever, Jensen!"

"I know what I am talking about."

"I am not so sure, and perhaps you are not sitting so securely in your office chair as you imagine. One of these days it may pitch you out without my having to say a single word to anybody."

"Thanks, I am getting on quite well without warnings. Give my love to Captain Schnell and tell him I like his face as little as he likes mine."

"Careful, Jensen."

"I hope he'll give you some more of his own fine tobacco and brandy so that you will have no need to envy the King."

At last the mayor reached the bursting point. His face went crimson, and he absolutely hissed.

"Jensen, you are the biggest rascal that has ever worked in this station. I hope the Gestapo will come one day and twist every joint in your body!"

After that he turned around and marched quickly away.

"See you again," shouted Jensen after him.

15 — Enter a Policeman

A pale, frozen half moon gave the only light there was when Bronna was led out of the stable the morning after Bergulv's party. The darkness of night still lay over the district, and there was as yet no sign of dawn behind the mountain ridge to the east.

Nothing is more depressing than a morning like this in December, thought Elling as, shivering, he crossed the farmyard, still half asleep, with Stepan beside him.

But Lars was awake and prepared.

"It's fine to have that moon," he said cheerfully. "Bronna is used to traveling in moonlight."

Elling yawned. "Oh yes, and anyhow it's better for us to get away before it's light."

"There's no danger here. Only good people live in this neighborhood. But we have a long drive in front of us."

Luckily the road was much smoother today, both for Bronna's sake and for the passengers. Bergulv had lent Lars a light sled that held everybody comfortably and was also easily drawn. Louisa had given them food and a Thermos full of hot coffee, as well as two lovely fur rugs.

"I won't have them leave this farm like tramps," she said laughingly as they said good-by. She gave Stepan one of her husband's huge woolen scarves, draping it comfortably around his head and ears.

Bronna jogged along steadily through narrow roads and by the shores of lakes. They traveled more quickly today, and Lars reckoned they should be in Hamar in good time, well before people began going to bed. Elling thought only of two things. One, what kind of lodgings they would be able to get in Hamar, and two, whether Captain Schnell had any spies out after Stepan there.

They had driven almost the whole day without any stop except for meals before he managed to bring himself to ask Lars.

"Listen, Lars, how shall we manage in Hamar, do you think?"

Lars cleared his throat. His pipe had gone out, for he had to ration his tobacco very strictly, and he had been silent for an hour.

"Well, I think you'll be all right," he answered. "Of course, there'll be no birthday party there."

"But kind people?"

"Not people—a man."

"Only one?"

"Yes. But Aslak should be more than enough."

"Do you know whether he will be at home?"

"That is just what I'm sitting here wondering."

Elling also fell silent, thinking his own thoughts. If the man was not at home, what then? Was there more trouble to be expected? He did not want more uncertainty and strain. He hoped from the bottom of his heart that they could get away for Elverum quickly and painlessly. Surely Lars would think of something.

After that, they did not talk about the future, only about the weather and yesterday's party.

Dusk fell quickly. Again they were driving in darkness, for the half moon was only visible now and again between heavy clouds. The frost creaked beneath the runners. Otherwise, the evening around them was quite silent.

A few miles farther on they heard—quite unexpectedly for Elling and Stepan—the sound of a car somewhere in the neighborhood, and immediately afterwards Lars turned up a little hill and said, "Here we are in Hamar."

This sounded quite incredible to his two passengers. They saw no sign of a town. Everything was blacked out, nor did they hear any sounds of people or vehicles.

Lars stopped the sled and asked them to wait a moment. They were at a cross road. A bus drove up, stopped, and suddenly the place was full of life. Many people streamed out, both with and without luggage. They saw the quick gleam of a flashlight, which shone for a moment on the well-polished uniform buttons of a man standing in front of the bus. A policeman had arrived, a Norwegian policeman as far as they could see.

The policeman allowed all those to pass who were empty-handed, only glancing at their identity cards, but he stopped all those who carried parcels and bags. He looked into the bags and opened some of the parcels while he only poked at others.

Instinctively, Elling felt for his identity card. Yes, it

was in his pocket. Stepan did the same and found his card with his name Anders Krooken.

What were they to think of this police check? It might be an ordinary check to find out whether people had been to the country to buy unrationed goods, such as meat, butter, eggs, and flour bought unlawfully on the Black Market. But it *could* be something else—for example, something with Captain Schnell behind it. Elling and Stepan did not feel at all safe as they sat there about fifty yards away from the control point.

Then they saw Lars go over and greet the policeman, even slap him on the shoulder. The policeman put his hand into his pocket and pulled out something that he gave Lars. Then he went on with his work.

Lars turned around. He was laughing silently when he came back to the sled.

"I haven't been so lucky for months, even years. Believe it or not, that was Aslak standing there brandishing his flashlight!"

"You mean the man we are to go to?"

"Exactly, and he's given me the key of his room."

Lars got onto the sled again, whipped up Bronna, and swung out into the main road. They had driven only a short way when he stopped again.

They were now right in the town, but in the blackout they could only see the street just close to them.

"Well, here I must leave you," he said. "I must go on and find stabling for Bronna. But first I must explain how you get to Aslak's home."

Lars explained, and then Elling helped Stepan out of the sled.

"Aren't you coming back, Lars?" he asked.

"No, I'll find lodging with the man who gives me stabling. Aslak will look after you. He'll soon be home. Here's the key."

Elling pulled off his glove and took Lar's hand.

"Good-by, Lars. I don't know . . . how I can . . . thank you." He began to stammer.

"Good-by, both of you. Good luck!" said Lars cheerfully.

Lars took Stepan's outstretched hand and shook it before he touched Bronna with the whip, and they disappeared into the darkness.

16 — Aslak

The entrance to which Lars had directed them was not many yards further along the street. They felt their way past the walls of the houses. "No matter how tiresome this blackout is," mumbled Elling to himself, "it is certainly useful for fugitives."

They found the entrance, went up a staircase, and opened a door without being seen by a single person. Elling had a brief glimpse of his surroundings from the weak light on the staircase. The house appeared to be an ordinary apartment house with three floors—old and very clean, but it obviously had not been painted for several years.

As a matter of fact, he tried to notice as little as possible, for the less he knew the better—in case they were caught.

He shivered; if only they could get to Elverum. . . . He did not dare think any further. The idea that he would ever get home again—to his mother, to Ingrid—seemed to him now like an impossible dream.

Aslak's home consisted of just one large room, furnished with a bed, a table, a cupboard, and an electric hot-plate, with two chairs and a washstand in one corner. In the other corner was a fireplace and a box half full of firewood. The rest was just open floor space—so large that a whole crowd of people could dance there, thought Elling lazily. Then he remembered that the Germans had forbidden dancing as well as many other things. They said that while German soldiers fought and died at the front, the Norwegian people should not be allowed to dance, and Aslak, who was a policeman, would be more than careful to do nothing unlawful—except to house fugitives!

Elling lit a small fire, and it burned quickly and well, warming the two frozen travelers. They sat down on the bed and waited, only daring to whisper to each other, not knowing how much could be heard through the walls.

Soon Stepan lay down. He did not complain with so much as a sound, but he looked as if his whole body was aching.

"You go to sleep," said Elling.

But Stepan shook his head. He would not think of going to sleep on the bed belonging to his benefactor. He only wanted to rest a little lying down as his muscles had become stiff from sitting so long in the sled. They both jumped when a little later the door opened and the firelight played on shining uniform buttons. But they realized at once that it was Aslak.

"Boo-oo-oo!" said Aslak, and he lifted his fists threateningly toward them. "Here comes a policeman to catch you both!"

Then he took off his uniform cap and smiled at them. He

was quite young and fair-haired and looked more like a helpful Boy Scout than a stern executive of the law.

"Good evening," said Elling. "Forgive us for jumping like that, but we didn't know for certain that it was you."

"Oh, there are many who jump when the police arrive." Aslak smiled. "Have you had any food?"

"Yes, a lot, and we still have some left."

"That's good because I have nothing."

"Here you are; eat some of ours!"

Aslak laughed. "Many thanks, but I am not hungry. I ate at the station and will have a new bread ration tomorrow."

He looked over at Stepan.

"There is a man who needs to rest. Move off the bed for a moment, and I'll arrange everything."

They moved, and Aslak got busy. He lifted up the quilt, the pillows, the sheets, and the mattress and rolled them all together at the end of the bed.

"Come along and help me," he said to Elling.

Greatly surprised, Elling now saw four or five mattresses, one lying on top of the other, together with a number of blankets—a complete layer of bedclothes. What did Aslak want all these for? It must mean he was used to hiding people. This was not so stupid—in fact, it was very clever because a policeman would be the last person to be suspected.

But one does not talk aloud about such things, and Elling began to help Aslak without asking any questions. They pulled out two mattresses and some blankets and made up a couple of beds for the fugitives. Stepan lay down immediately and gave a long sigh of contentment.

Aslak looked at the clock.

"Yes, there isn't much else we can do except go to bed now," he said. "I have to be on duty early tomorrow morning, and you are going on to Elverum, aren't you?"

"Yes, but we don't know how. We do not dare use the railway or the bus."

"Well, no doubt we'll be able to arrange something, but it's difficult for me to get anything done for you before the afternoon."

Elling thought.

"I can perhaps go out into the village early in the morning and scout around a bit," he suggested. "After all, there is nothing suspicious about me."

Aslak looked a little doubtful. He had to think over this suggestion for a few minutes.

"There may be something in what you say," he then said. "One never knows what chances may turn up. Were you thinking of a timber driver or something like that?"

"Yes, why not?" Elling, sitting here securely in a warm room, began to feel bolder and more experienced.

"All right," Aslak agreed. "Go, but be careful that you are not noticed."

"You can depend on me."

"And if you should by any chance get into any trouble, you know where to find me."

"Yes, that's fine."

Aslak nodded but suddenly thought of something else.

"Oh," he said. "Now I think of it—it's Sunday tomorrow."

"Oh," said Elling, disappointed. "I didn't remember that."

"Well, you can take a little walk around anyhow."

"All right, I will."

A sound from one of the mattresses made them turn around. Stepan had fallen asleep. He lay on his back, fully dressed and snoring.

"Hush, don't wake him," said Aslak in a whisper. "That poor beggar needs all the sleep he can get."

Elling spread a blanket over him. "Sleep well, Uncle Anders. I hope we'll be lucky tomorrow."

17 — Strange Fellow Travelers

Aslak had been up and out of the house for a long time before Elling got up the next morning, although it was still dark. Stepan was already awake, feeling much better after his long rest. They made their coffee on Aslak's stove and found that they had enough food left for breakfast in the parcel Louisa had given them.

Outside, the dawn was slowly breaking. They drew aside the blackout curtains and were rewarded with a tiny ray of sunlight while they ate.

Stepan was not so smiling as usual. He had a sad and anxious look on his face. He seemed to be thinking about something definite, something he found difficult to express in the mixed language they used between them, but a little later he got it out.

Elling was taking too great risks for his sake, he said; his life was not worth all this.

Elling protested. "All lives are valuable, whether they are Norwegian or Russian or even of a nation whose name had better not be mentioned."

But, Stepan went on, a sick man might never be able to get all that long way to Sweden alive. They must not bother about him any more. Too many people had exposed themselves to danger for his sake already.

"But do you want us to kill you straight away?" asked Elling.

A sick man's death in the middle of a world war, said Stepan calmly, was of no consequence. He was not at all afraid to die, and actually he thought it would be much better for everyone if he were now left to his own devices.

"Not to be thought of," said Elling decidedly. All this talk about death made him restless and depressed. He did not want to hear any more of it. Now he was going out to *do* something instead of sitting here talking.

He asked Stepan kindly to keep all this death talk to himself. Hadn't they gotten on fine up to this moment?

Yes, they had.

Now he, Elling, was going out to see if he could find some more luck for them.

He pulled on his boots quickly, put on his parka, and rushed out of the room. Stepan could do nothing but stay where he was, shaking his head as he followed Elling with his eyes.

To Elling, the village seemed more dead than alive, but then he would not have expected anything else so early on a Sunday morning in December. He was not known in Hamar and sauntered through a couple of streets at random. A dog and two young boys with skates hanging around their necks were the only sign of life he encountered. Not much hope of finding their big stroke of luck here it seemed. It would have been much better if it had been a day in the middle of the week.

Then he heard an unexpected kind of sound—the sound of drums. Had he heard aright? Drums! That seemed very odd. It must be something out of the ordinary, for it was about the time the church bells ought to begin ringing, and surely drums would not be allowed then.

Therefore, it must be the Germans. They were the masters here in the country, so that their troops could drum and sing and march as much and whenever it suited them.

It would be best to keep at a distance. But the Germans were never dangerous when they were playing music or that sort of thing. He might even go a little nearer and have a look. Surely there could be no harm in trying to get a little amusement on a dull morning in this quiet village. He walked slowly in the direction of the sound.

At the end of the street he swung around a corner and suddenly found himself in the marketplace. This was where the drumming came from.

But it was not made by German soldiers. In the middle of the square stood a large bus decorated with little yellow and red swastika flags. Boys of all ages crowded around the bus, dressed in the uniform of the Hitler Youth movement. There were some girls there, too, also in uniform.

Two of the boys were drumming. It looked as if they were gathering to go by bus to some place or other.

Elling glanced over the rest of the square. On the opposite side was a policeman in uniform. Why, it was Aslak.

He was no doubt standing there to keep order, for there was often trouble when the Hitler Youth were out and about in Norway.

Aslak noticed Elling almost at the same moment. He made a slight movement of the head, and Elling understood: Aslak wanted him to go away. As a policeman, he had no doubt been in conflict with the Hitler Youth before now, and he did not want to risk Elling's being involved in anything of that sort. Elling nodded to Aslak and turned to go back.

Then suddenly one of the older boys came toward him.

Elling pretended not to notice and began walking quickly away from the square. The boy began to run, and Elling increased his pace.

"Hi, Elling!" he heard from behind him.

Elling stopped immediately. There seemed to be something familiar in the voice, and sure enough, the boy was none other than Torjus, one of his schoolmates from his old home district! Torjus had been one class above him.

This meeting was a shock. Elling had had no idea that Torjus had joined the Hitler Youth movement and was actually in a troop. But there stood the friend of his childhood dressed in a black Hitler Youth uniform with a crooked cross plastered on it here and there.

But Torjus had always been a gentle, nondescript sort of boy. Impossible that he could be dangerous.

"Hello, Torjus," said Elling. "I didn't know that it was you."

Torjus beamed just as in the old days.

"No, I don't suppose you knew anything about this," he said and by way of amusement made the Nazi salute.

Elling kept back the words that were on his tongue, but he must have shown a little of what he felt, for Torjus no longer beamed as broadly as before.

"It's a long time since we've seen each other, Torjus," Elling hastened to say.

"Yes, a couple of years at least. How are you getting on up there inland?"

"Not too badly. And you still live in the same place?"

"Yes, but now we're out on a propaganda trip."

"Where are you going in this bus?"

"To Elverum. To a large Hitler Youth rally, but this afternoon we are going on to Kongsvinger."

Elling's pulses began to beat faster. Was this his chance? To drive in a bus reserved for Nazi youth would probably be the safest conveyance he could possibly find!

"The bolder the better"! No Germans would make a raid on a Hitler Youth bus—not even Captain Schnell.

He would take the chance.

"So you're going to Elverum," Elling remarked, trying to seem only slightly interested. "Why, I'm going there myself."

"You don't say! Come in our bus. There's plenty of room, and you'll get a free ride."

"Thanks a lot—but I'm not alone."

"Are there many of you?"

"Only one more."

"Then that will be fine. Who is it anyhow?"

"Oh well . . . it's my uncle . . . Uncle Anders. He's old and sick unfortunately."

"Is he going to Elverum, too?

"Yes, he is . . . to an old men's home there," Elling said in his hurry, and immediately he realized how stupid he'd been. He had no idea whether there was an old men's home in Elverum or whether, if there had been, it was among those houses that had been bombed in 1940. But now he had said it, and he must take his chance. After all, Torjus was not known there and would have other things to think of than old men's homes when they arrived. How lucky for them that the Nazi youth people were going on to Kongsvinger!

"All in order. Go and fetch the old man," said Torjus good-naturedly. "We're off in a quarter of an hour."

"Fine—I'll run!"

And Elling ran. A quarter of an hour later he sat with "the old man" in the bus among all the Nazi youth. The bus started up and swung into the road leading to Elverum. The uniformed passengers sang at the tops of their voices, "Forward, Quisling Warriors!" leaving a police officer standing in the square who made a satisfied grimace at the back of the receding bus.

108

18 — Ingrid Feels Lonely

Ingrid had been mostly alone after Elling had gone to the "hospital." During the days leading up to the fateful Thursday all was well, for then she was excited and nervous, but after all was over, it became worse and worse to have no one in whom she could confide. She felt exceedingly lonely.

She had no idea when Elling would be coming back. She did not like to visit Jensen, for she was certain that he would not be very pleased if she came to see him unnecessarily. She also kept herself well away from Willie for security's sake. She managed to get some parcels of food smuggled into the Russian camp now and again but through other sentries. They were all nervous and very, very careful since Stepan's flight. Captain Schnell was not nice to have anything to do with these days, one of them told her. He raged about and reprimanded people for nothing at all. He had, besides, threatened to shoot ten of the prisoners if he failed to catch Stepan.

On Sunday morning Ingrid went for a ski trip alone. She followed the ski run that she and Elling used to take, which led to a peak in the neighborhood. There she could at least pretend that she was talking to someone.

The weather was fine and clear; the same sun shone over her as over Elling and Stepan down in Hamar. She dug her ski sticks into the snow and like a dancer glided lightly forward over the silky surface of the snow-covered fields. A little later she entered the forest and began climbing upward. Suddenly she stopped, shading her eyes with her gloved hand. In the sharp sunshine she saw a man standing waiting for her. He was on skis too, a good-looking figure in a green German uniform, a well-cut, well-pressed Sunday uniform. It was Willie.

"Hello, Ingrid," he called in his foreigner's Norwegian. "I thought you might be coming this way."

"But, Willie, you can't do this," she reproached him. "You can't meet me here."

"Why not?"

"It's the middle of the day. People may come past at any moment."

"What does it matter?"

"But you must know that I can't stand here talking to a German soldier. They will call me a 'Boche girl' immediately."

"But don't they realize that you know me?" Willie pretended he did not understand her properly.

"But can't you see it's quite different when we take food packages to the Russians. But standing here talking—you must see—it looks almost as if we were sweethearts."

110

Surprised and irritated with herself, Ingrid blushed when she said this. Willie looked at her, and he also blushed. She saw the intense look in his dark brown eyes and blushed still more.

"No, we can't stay here!" she said quickly and tried to go on past him.

But Willie took hold of her arm.

"We'll go a little to the side here. I must speak to you."

Ingrid hesitated. She could not deny that she felt inclined to talk to him and also that he deserved it. Not many Germans would have helped them as Willie had done. But then there was all the gossip to be reckoned with.

"Sh-sh . . ." Could she not hear the tap-tap of ski sticks in the forest? Was anyone coming?

That settled it. She turned on her skis and went straight in through the fir trees away from the ski run.

"Follow me!" she cried to Willie.

He followed her slowly and carefully, for he had not known how to ski before he came over to Norway.

Ingrid did not stop until she was certain that she was at a good distance from all curious eyes and ears. Willie came slowly along behind, and she was obliged to laugh when she saw how clumsy he was. He was panting and sweating as if he had been on a long trip when at last he reached her.

"Phew," he groaned. "Norwegian girls are not so easy to follow when they are out in the open."

"At any rate, not in winter!" Ingrid laughed.

111

He stood panting, and it was some time before he got his breath again. Then he asked, "How is Elling getting on in the hospital?"

"Quite well, thank you. He'll soon be home," lied Ingrid.

"When is he coming back?"

"I don't know exactly."

Willie looked away; then he cleared his throat a little awkwardly. Suddenly Ingrid remembered that she had not seen him since that dramatic night. She pulled off her right glove and stretched out her hand.

"Thanks for your help, Willie."

"Don't speak of it again," he said hesitatingly, but he pulled off his glove and grasped her hand eagerly, nor would he let it go.

"You," he began a minute later, "are . . . are you . . . very fond . . . of Elling?"

"We've been friends for a long, long time."

"Are you . . . are you going to get married?"

Ingrid giggled nervously.

"We are too young to think of that yet."

Willie cleared his throat awkwardly again; then he suddenly lifted her hand and kissed it. Once again he stared right into her eyes.

"I want to tell you," he said in a voice that had suddenly become deep and firm, "that you have the prettiest hair and the prettiest eyes I have ever seen."

She looked at him a little suspiciously, trying to find out if he were only teasing her. But his face was altogether honest and serious, and the love in his eyes shone out as clearly as if it had been written. She smiled.

"And the prettiest smile, too," he added.

Ingrid blushed again. Willie did not blush, for he had become more sure of himself.

No longer did she feel quite so superior on her skis; his deep voice and the flattering words made her tremble just a little. She was so unaccustomed to this—he had even kissed her hand! It made her picture of Elling seem tame and childish. Willie was over twenty years old, a fully-grown man, good-looking, dark-haired, not unlike a film hero. His uniform made him still more splendid.

Willie was in love with her, and he said so both with his eyes and in his charming foreign accent. He stood here paying her compliments as if she were his opposite in a romantic movie. He kissed her hand as gallantly as a cavalier.

No, this must not go on. She pulled her hand quickly away and forced herself to laugh.

"We must go home, and quite separate ways, Willie."

"Wait a minute. I have some chocolate for you."

He pulled out a large slab of chocolate and gave it to her. This she could not resist. She had not tasted chocolate for about a year. Greedily she ate the whole piece while he stood watching her. He did not try to hide the fact that he had quite as much feeling for her as she had for the chocolate.

"Thank you, thank you," she said. "Bad Germans who steal our chocolate."

"It's not my fault."

"Perhaps not. But now I must go!"

He held her back.

"I'm on guard in the camp tomorrow evening. Will you be coming with a parcel?"

"Perhaps."

"Sure?"

"All right."

She pulled herself away from him and disappeared with quick strokes of her ski sticks. She had to run far before the sweet quivering inside her had quite passed.

19 — Peter

In Elverum the bus stopped on the west side of the river. Lucky again, thought Elling, for there, just in front of him, lay the station. On the east side, there were not many houses left there after the bombing in 1940.

During the latter part of the journey in the bus, Elling had sat beside Stepan whispering, "Now we are on historic ground. This is the way King Haakon fled with his followers two and a half years ago. He had the German troops at his heels all the way. Over there the enemy was halted by Norwegian bullets at a bend in the road. Then they bombed Elverum in an attempt to catch the King there. Many were killed, but not the one they were after."

They saw evident traces of the bombing far away through the window of the bus.

The two civilian passengers were last to leave the bus. Torjus was so busy instructing the smaller Hitler boys that he had no time for anything except to say good-by. "The old man" was not mentioned again.

Elling went straight to the station. Stepan walked slowly beside him, his back bent, each step an effort. He was very stiff after the long drive. Just before they got to the station, Elling asked him to wait.

Inside the station everything appeared locked up and deserted. The Express Goods Department seemed to be shut. There was only one solitary railway employee to be seen clearing ice from the lines.

There seemed no one else for Elling to ask, so he had to take a chance. He jumped down from the platform.

The man gave him a mild good morning, but his face grew closed and expressionless when Elling asked for Peter.

"I don't know anyone called Peter," he mumbled.

"That's—that's very odd," said Elling, bewildered.

"Indeed?" The man turned around and continued hacking at the ice.

Goodness, now I have done something wrong, thought Elling. Obviously this man does not belong to the station staff. I only hope he is not a Nazi, for if so, I shall be in the soup. But I will try once more.

"I have greetings from Jensen," he said, suddenly remembering the most important part of the operation. "It was he who sent me here."

The man looked at him now without the slightest trace of sulkiness.

"Are you alone?" he asked.

"No, I have a friend outside."

"Someone who wants—a lift?"

"Exactly."

"Come with me."

The employee put down his tools and went in front of

Elling onto the platform and out of the station. Once there, he pointed in a definite direction.

"Go down there and turn right at the first corner. Unless I am mistaken, Peter is there now with his car. Look for a gray-covered truck with a wood generator. Good luck," he added.

Then he turned quickly and went back to the station again. Elling had just time to shout after him, "Thanks a lot!"

He fetched Stepan, and they went along the road that the station employee had pointed out. They swung to the right around the corner—and there stood the gray-covered truck with a wood generator. A man was filling up the generator with logs from a paper sack. Black smoke was whirling up, and the man's face was as black as that of a coal heaver. That must be Peter.

Elling mounted the step so as to get as near the man as possible.

"Greetings from Jensen," he said in a whisper.

"Thank you."

Peter continued to load up the wood without turning around.

"I was to ask whether you could drive us to Stølen."

Peter grunted and coughed in the smoke and rummaged about in the container with a stick. At last he said, "Are you in a hurry?"

"We are already two days late."

"Two days, that's nothing. There's a war on! Can't you wait until Wednesday?"

"We have nowhere to live. It's dangerous for us to be

out in the daylight as the Germans are looking for us, and this man is ill, too." Elling pointed to Stepan.

"I have nowhere to put you up nowadays," said Peter. "There are no vacant rooms in Elverum, as you can see."

"We can sleep on camp beds."

"Yes, of course, but there is no floor space for camp beds."

"Can't we put up in the back of the truck?"

Peter laughed harshly.

"It's not easy to get rid of you two. Jump up behind then and sit there quietly until it gets dark. Then there won't be much spare room, I promise you."

"Shall we be leaving then?"

"We'll leave as soon as it's dark. In you get."

Elling swung himself up onto the tailboard and helped Stepan up. They crept right in as far as they could go under the covering and sat down. From now on, according to Peter's instructions, they only whispered when they spoke.

They heard Peter struggling with the difficult generator outside. He spat out soot and cursed the war, which made it impossible for an honest chauffeur to get fuel for his car and forced him to use such miserable stuff as wood. But eventually he finished and climbed down. A minute later he put his sooty head into the truck and said, "So Jensen sent his love. How is he?"

"Fine, I think."

"Has he sent you with the necessary equipment?"

"I think we have all we need."

"Food? Skis? Money?"

"He said that the money will be coming. We have finished our food now. He mentioned nothing about skis."

"Ha, ha, the good man! All is in order. There are skis and plenty of food at Stølen. See you later. Good-by."

Peter disappeared, and they sat there waiting again.

But Elling was full of relief and joy—the last stage of the journey had begun or, at any rate, the next to last. And from now on he would not have to chase blindly after people to help him.

20 — More Fugitives

Dusk had only just begun to fall when Peter came back, but the light farthest in under the roof of the truck soon disappeared as he began to stack up some large cases and sacks right at the back. There was another man with him, and they finished the job in a few minutes. Neither of them spoke while they were loading.

It was quite dark where Elling and Stepan were sitting, but there was plenty of room all around them, so they wondered what Peter could have meant when he said they would not have much room.

The two men outside began to deal with the very complicated job of getting the engine to start. After a great deal of noise and creaking they succeeded, and with a sudden jump the truck began to move forward.

"Now we are driving across the Glomma," whispered Elling to Stepan after a short time. He thought he could hear the hollow sound of the bridge beneath them. "On the other side there are only naked chimneys, for the Germans bombed the town to bits. Pity we can't see it."

"I've seen quite enough of bombed towns and cities to last me a lifetime," Stepan replied. "The whole Ukraine is full of naked chimneys."

"Sorry, I never thought of that. I suppose the Germans have ruined your country entirely!"

"Forget it, Elling. We are in Norway now. The war is a misfortune for us all."

For a time they drove on in silence. Elling sat there brooding.

"Stepan," he said at last, "can you imagine why Peter said we should be so crowded in here?"

"Perhaps we'll have more passengers."

"But we must be right out in the country!"

"How do I know!"

They had no need to speculate much longer for the truck suddenly swung around and stopped. They heard Peter's voice, and he and his assistant came around and pushed a couple of cases to one side. By now it was quite dark outside.

Peter put a lantern just inside the truck.

"Now you'll have company," he said shortly. "Pull yourselves together and be friends."

The two men seemed to be struggling with something out in the dark, and then they heard Peter's voice again.

"Come and help here, boy—help us pile up." Elling came forward at once.

First a couple of skis tied together were thrust into his arms. He put them in position and was given two more. After that his arms were filled with ski sticks. Everything came to him so quickly and unexpectedly that he had no time to think.

Next followed in quick succession rucksacks, sleeping bags, and other baggage. The light from the lantern was right in his eyes, so that Elling could not see far enough to distinguish the people behind all these possessions. He suspected that the truck was standing in front of a house, but that was all. Besides, he had enough to do in stowing away the things he was given. Stepan helped as well as he could. The space where they had been sitting grew smaller and smaller.

Finally there was no more room at all.

"Look out! The living baggage is coming in now!" Peter warned them.

If the two passengers had not been surprised before, they were so now. The first to be helped up was a mother with a sleeping child in her arms. The child could not have been more than a year old. What wrong could these two have done the Germans? Why was a mother with a sleeping child in her arms obliged to flee in the very darkest night? Elling could not understand.

Next another woman arrived, this time with three older children, a boy of ten or twelve and two girls who were perhaps a little older. Finally came two men. They must be two families, thought Elling, and they were obviously fleeing, leaving all they had behind them except this luggage here. None of them looked dangerous or suspicious or as if they were carrying on something secret or playing a double game. They seemed to be as ordinary and peaceful as anyone could be.

Elling did not want to be inquisitive; it was absolutely against all that Jensen had taught him, but he could not help it. He longed to know why these people were fleeing the country. But he did not dare ask.

Peter was right—there was now not much room in the truck. They had to crowd together if they wanted to sit down, and there was scarcely an inch in which to move about. It was no good even trying to stretch their legs or change their positions. They sat as if they were glued together, breathing into each other's faces—all in complete darkness.

Where were they going? How long would it take? From whatever angle you looked at it, this was certainly not a pleasure trip.

The first hour or so passed with nerve-racking slowness but with no hindrance or disaster. There was not a sound in the darkness except that of everybody's breathing and the chug-chug of the engine. No one in the crowd uttered a sound. No doubt they all sat there with their hearts in their mouths, frightened and yet full of desperate hope.

The truck suddenly slowed down. The noise of an approaching motorcycle reached them. The truck stopped, and Peter shut off the engine. Those inside heard several motorcycles and cars coming nearer, all driven on proper fuel. They heard German voices shouting words of command. Inside the truck the sound of breathing came more and more quickly.

There was no doubt about it. They had met a German military column, and all now depended on what mission this column was performing and how zealous and curious the officers were.

Peter was on his guard. He had gotten out of the driver's seat, and they heard him shout politely in German to every vehicle that passed. It was important not to annoy them in any way whatsoever. From his calm, assured tone of voice, his passengers understood that this was not the first time that he had been in such a predicament.

The road was quiet again, and Peter started up once more. A man's voice in the darkness sighed deeply and said, "Thank God." A woman's voice answered with a sob, "Yes, thank God." Several sighs of relief were heard until a voice broke the tense silence and said, "There is no reason why we should not talk aloud; no one can hear us while we are moving."

"But won't it wake the child?" someone else asked.

"It has been given sleeping pills."

Now the older children began to talk eagerly. They spoke of their happy expectations of what they would get when they reached Sweden, of the good food—eggs, cream, meat, jam, chocolate, white bread, and lots of sweet things.

The adults had to tell them to be quiet. "Don't speak too soon children. The danger is not over yet."

The grownups talked a little, too, but only hesitatingly and about the weather and their clever driver. No real conversation was started. There was anxiety and nervousness beneath the surface.

No one dared speak freely, for they did not know each other.

The road grew worse and worse. The truck bumped along, taking sharp corners, and sometimes it felt as if they were driving over roots and even stumps of trees in the forest itself. None of the passengers knew what route they were taking and no one wished to know. Escape routes must be kept strictly secret. They meant life or death to more and more Norwegians who were obliged to flee. Many thousands had already fled, and if the Germans were to get a suspicion of any of the secret roads, it would mean catastrophe.

Nevertheless, the whole nation knew that there were many such routes to the Swedish border, and no doubt Peter's passengers sat in the darkness speculating as to where on the map they were now. Elling, too, tried to figure out their whereabouts and thought they must be somewhere in the Finn forest. But he would not mention this to a single living soul—not until the war was over.

The engine strained and strained. Peter shifted into first gear, and the truck began climbing slowly upward, but it moved more and more slowly and the wood generator coughed and spluttered. Then the wheels began to lose their grip. The road was too slippery—and then the truck stopped altogether.

Peter gave up and applied the hand brake. His assistant went to the back, lifted a case to one side, and shouted, "All able-bodied men come out and push!"

He did not need to speak twice. The men and the two boys jumped out of the truck at top speed. To be able to stretch their legs and move about made them feel almost as if they had been released from a torture chamber. The engine began to strain again, and they all pushed. The wheels gripped, and the truck moved up the slope yard by yard.

21 — Under Sentence of Death

The moon had risen in the evening sky, and it shone with a ghostly whiteness over the magic and deserted forest landscape. They were deep in the wilderness in the black, legendary Finn forest. The road beneath them looked as if it were nothing but an old rugged timber track. At one place they bumped over a heap of frozen horse dung. This route was much better suited to a sled than to modern motor vehicles.

Elling was pushing beside the other boy. The truck moved easily now, and they scarcely had to push at all. The two boys walked side by side looking at each other, both of them longing to talk but neither knowing quite how to begin.

Elling thought that it was better not to tell him anything. He is so much younger than I am. I don't think he could keep a secret.

But then the other suddenly asked, "Are you a Jew?"

"Me? No!" Elling answered, amazed.

"Nor the old man either?"

"No."

"That is strange. I was almost certain that he was one, at any rate."

"No, but are you?"

"Only half Jew. My mother is a Jewess, and the father of the two little girls, too. Otherwise, there is only Norwegian blood in our families."

"Is that why . . . ?"

"Yes, the Germans are taking us all now, whether we are whole or half or quarter, and sometimes even less."

Elling was startled. Now he remembered that he had read last autumn in one of the secret newspapers that all Jews in Norway were to be arrested and sent to Germany—men, women, and children. In Germany they were collected in special concentration camps—camps for Jews from all the countries in Europe that were occupied by the Germans. There was not much hope of getting away from those dreadful camps. They were called "extermination camps," Elling remembered. Hitler had ordered that the Jewish race should be exterminated. If these two families were caught during their flight, they would be sent to such a camp and killed, even the little child who now lay sleeping.

He said, his voice quite weak, "You're lucky to have gotten away."

"We were warned in advance by the Underground," answered the boy, "and were hidden in Oslo for several weeks before we came up here."

"Do you know anyone who—who was taken?"

"My mother's sister and her children. Some other relations, too. I think there are many hundreds who have not been able to flee."

The boy was silent, and Elling asked no more. The thought of the fate that awaited all arrested Jews—the fate that his fellow travelers still risked—took from him all desire to talk.

The truck rolled onto flat ground again, and all those who had been pushing had a rest for a short way. When they came to the next hill, they had to get out again and push. They went on like this, flat stretches and hills, one after the other, and the passengers had no objection to the change.

The moon followed them; the forest seemed less oppressively deserted as long as it shone.

Hours passed. They had not met a living soul (thank God!) since the German column on the high road. They almost dared to feel safe, deep in the forest as they were and so far away from people.

Therefore, it seemed almost unreal, like a dream, when after turning a corner, a bunch of small gray houses came into view. But the houses were real enough. They had reached Stølen!

Only an hour later Elling sat in the truck on his way back. His stay in Stølen had been much shorter than he had expected. The other passengers were anxious to put on their skis and go on toward the Swedish frontier immediately. Peter had almost to threaten them before they would agree to rest for a while and eat a little food before they started off. Then it was discovered that one of the fugitives was a doctor. He examined Stepan and said that it would be a long time before he would be well enough to go on. It was quite impossible for him to make this very demanding journey across the frontier at present, said the doctor. If he did so, he would probably collapse altogether. He must go to bed immediately and stay there for at least a fortnight.

The old couple in Stølen, the only people there, immediately offered to keep him with them and look after him. Peter told Elling that he must report this information to Jensen, as then Jensen would decide how best Uncle Anders could be helped further.

As for Peter, he would not allow himself any time for a rest because he was too busy with refugee transport at the moment. He must get back to his own district as soon as the goods destined for Stølen were unpacked.

Everybody stayed out in the yard and watched the two condemned families set off on the last part of their trip toward freedom. They would have a difficult time with their heavy baggage. The men were going to take turns carrying the youngest child.

Stepan found it difficult to smile as he said good-by to his traveling companion.

"People are doing too much for me," he complained again, "but I will never forget anybody."

"Good luck, Stepan!"

22 — Meeting with Ingrid

Ingrid went to the Russian camp late on Monday evening with a bag of food. It was dark, and she met nobody on the way.

Nowadays food parcels were more welcome than ever. The camp food had become steadily worse. Food supplies were greatly reduced, even for the Norwegians, so it was not very often that they had anything to give away.

In addition, the guards said that Captain Schnell had reduced the prisoners' rations in his fury and was coming as near to starving them as he dared.

Ingrid was therefore always delighted when she had "give-away-food" in her bag. She took a warm delight in these trips, but tonight the joy had something else mixed up with it, something she did not wish to admit. However, she felt quite proud of the way she had handled the situation yesterday.

Willie stood on guard outside the gate. He took a few steps and then turned his back while she threw the parcels over the fence to the nearest prisoner, who disappeared into a barrack with them. Willie came toward her and held out his hand. Teasingly she put her hands behind her back.

"Good evening, beautiful princess," he said.

"Good evening, wicked wolf."

He laughed softly.

"And yet you dare to come to the wicked wolf?"

"I didn't come to the wolf. I came with food for the lambs."

"You're very stupid to think they are lambs."

"And you are very stupid to think you're better than they are."

"Well, don't let's speak about them." He came nearer and took hold of her hands, but she twisted herself away.

"No more nonsense now or I'll go home at once," she said, threatening him.

"Don't do that. I've brought some more chocolate for you tonight."

He patted his uniform pocket but did not pull out the chocolate.

"Idiot," she answered, "you can't buy a Norwegian girl with chocolate!"

Willie sighed. He was very impressed by her pat answers and stood staring at her, admiring her in the weak light from the moon, which at that moment rose up over the treetops.

"Do you know what, little princess?" he said. "You are just as lovely in the moonlight as in the sunlight."

He smiled, and his row of fine white pearly teeth shone

under his steel helmet (an absolutely new steel helmet, which also shone).

"Thank you, chocolate prince!" You're not bad either, she thought, but did not say so aloud.

They stood there for a time, he paying her compliments and she teasing him, but that she liked to hear the nice words neither he nor she doubted any longer.

At last he became tired of her teasing, took hold of her shoulders, and shook her playfully.

"Look up at me," he commanded her, "and keep that sweet little mouth of yours still for a moment."

She looked up at him, and his eyes were dangerously close to hers now. There was a fire in them that she could not fail to understand.

"Can't you see that I'm serious," he said with a slight tremble in his voice. "I'm really in love with you."

Now she felt the trembling in her worse than yesterday, worse than she had ever felt it. She turned her face away from his shining eyes and hot breath.

"You—you must not be in love with me. It is no good— you see."

"All right. But I must steal a kiss from you all the same!"

He pressed her to him so suddenly and so powerfully that she could not make much resistance. She tried to defend herself while he kissed her, but she also felt this was a kiss in the best tradition of the movies, wild and romantic with the moon as sole witness. She fought against him with her eyes open, so she could not avoid seeing that

132

the moon was not, after all, the only witness. Suddenly she saw something more than the shadows of the trees on the road, a shadow that made quite another picture against the snow—the shadow of a person, the person she loved the most in the world.

She pulled herself violently away and shouted, "Elling!"

But the shadow had disappeared, and she heard his running steps in the darkness, taking a short cut through the forest.

"Elling! Wait!"

She ran after the marks of his boots. They sank deep into the snow; he ran more heavily than she did. She stopped for a moment and called.

"Don't be stupid, Elling! Wait!"

He ran a few more steps, and then he waited for her. By this time they were almost out on the main road again at the end of the path.

Ingrid drew a deep breath before she could say anything.

"How wonderful that you have come back, Elling, but there is nothing for you to be angry at!"

"Isn't there? Well, what was it I saw then!" said Elling moodily.

"You thought you saw something more than you did!"

"You have kissed a German, Ingrid!"

"That I have never done!"

"Don't deny it. I saw it."

"Then you saw wrong. Don't you know that he took that kiss by force?"

"Well, you didn't seem to have anything against it!"

"Elling—how can you say that!"

"Why, you were standing there flirting with him!"

Ingrid felt anger rising in her.

"Elling, you know why I was there. I had my bag full of food. And you stood there spying on me. Shame on you!"

But Elling felt no need to feel ashamed of himself. On the contrary, he felt hurt and offended and dreadfully disappointed. He had been longing, like a little boy, to tell all his adventures to Ingrid. He had felt like a soldier coming back from the firing line, coming home to his sweetheart. He had grudged his mother a bare half hour to rejoice in his return before he went to meet Ingrid. He had never been so full of expectation in his life before.

When he saw her standing there flirting with Willie, he had felt quite brutal. There was a threatening lump in his throat that hindered him from going forward to them at once. It was this that kept him standing there hidden and "spying."

They walked along side by side now without saying anything. It was a miserable meeting, a sad disappointment for both of them, and they needed time to pull themselves together and face up to it. But Elling had to clear himself of her last accusation.

"I was not spying, Ingrid," he said violently. "I can't explain anything more to you."

"No, go and sulk as much as you like. I don't care," Ingrid snapped.

Now they were enemies. They walked homeward side

by side, but both of them were deeply offended. After they had gone a little way in silence, Ingrid could not help asking, "Tell me how things went with Stepan."

"No."

"Why not?"

"I won't tell anyone but those—those I can trust."

He could not have said anything worse. This time it was Ingrid who was brutally wounded and who felt a lump in her throat.

"Oh, Elling, you are a—you are worse than a German," she shouted at him and ran away.

He did not follow her. She ran straight home.

23 — Report

Elling went to the station to give his report to Jensen. The telegraph clerk had not been on duty when Elling's train had arrived, so he hoped to see Jensen now. Yes, he was in his office.

"Well, there you are at last, comrade," Jensen shouted. "I've sat here imagining all sorts of disasters ever since the absurd difficulty with the freight train. How is your earache?"

"Not so bad."

"Sit down and tell me all about it!"

Elling sat down and told him. Jensen put a cigarette stub into his holder and smoked intensely while he listened. Now and again he thrummed on the table with his fingers and said "Fine!" or "Splendid!" He laughed loudly when Elling told him about the journey in the Hitler Youth bus from Hamar to Elverum.

"As good as if I'd done it myself!" He laughed. "You'll be a major general in the Underground yet—if the war lasts long enough."

But Elling admitted, "I don't want to go on an expedition like that again, Jensen."

Jensen nodded. "Don't take me too literally, comrade. It's all the very devil, but at last there seems to be a hope that it may be coming to an end. Continue about Uncle Anders!"

Elling told him about the last lap—the drive up to Stølen and about the doctor who had examined Stepan.

"I half expected something of the sort," said Jensen. "At any rate, I had reckoned that he would have to stay in Stølen for a time, poor man. How they plagued him!"

"But what now? Who is to take him across the border?"

"I myself! I have a few days' leave still due me, and I could not use them better than by seeing the prisoner well over into freedom. He deserves it. We shall never get his equal sawing wood for the railway again."

"Perhaps there may be other refugees to help him across —some Jews for example," Elling suggested carefully.

"Not very likely. And, anyway, I should like to help him myself. I'll send a message to Stølen about it."

"Uncle Anders will be tremendously pleased when he gets it."

"I will personally see to it that he eats his Christmas dinner in Sweden." Now Jensen looked intently at his co-helper. "But you don't look especially happy, Elling. Have you lost your butter ration card, or what is it?"

"Nothing," muttered Elling, feeling himself blush.

"Aha, you are blushing! Something with Ingrid then?" Elling did not answer.

"I'll tell you one thing, my boy," Jensen went on. "Ingrid is the bravest girl who ever walked in a pair of shoes in this part of the country. Without her help we could never have gotten the man out of his cage at all. Put that in your pipe and smoke it!" Elling still said nothing.

Jensen cleared his throat and thumped him on the back.

"I understand," he said in a fatherly tone. "There is nothing like a real, tight knot in the thread now and again. Down into the deepest, darkest pit of sorrow and misery for days—and then a leap up into seventh heaven!" He jumped up into the air from the office floor and came down again with such a thump that it made the telephone bell tinkle.

"But of course you don't believe me," he added.

"No," answered Elling bluntly.

"Well, well, tell Ingrid for me that all is in order. I must go now because a train is due. Thanks for a wonderful report! Good-by."

"Good-by, Jensen."

24 — Captain Schnell Strikes Again

In a lunch break at school the following day, Ingrid walked up and down the schoolyard with Teddy, a boy who was both taller and better-looking than Elling. She chattered to him so busily that she had no time to look either to right or to left.

Elling, for his part, stood in the middle of a group of boys and boasted of the time he had had in the "hospital."

Apparently neither of them noticed that the other one existed, although this was the break they usually spent together. If Jensen had seen them, he would probably have enjoyed the sight and would have congratulated them on their good acting. Perhaps he might even have made them laugh. But Jensen was not there, so their game went on. They both hid their unhappiness beneath a mask of indifference.

This state of things did not last for only a day. They went on wearing their masks for a whole week. The Christmas holidays were approaching, and it looked almost as if they were going to stay enemies right over Christmas.

Ingrid went to the prison camp regularly, delivering parcels, and this did not make Elling feel any better. She also went up to Jensen once, and he gave her a short account of what Elling had refused to tell her. She was not going to make up to anyone who did not trust her.

She kept company with Teddy, while Elling stayed with his classmates, for he was not the type who could flirt easily. In reality he was shy and helpless in the company of girls, except of course with Ingrid, so he suffered a good deal during this time, probably more than Ingrid really meant him to suffer. He was not only wounded but also jealous and secretly envious.

This tense and strange condition between them could not last forever, that was obvious. But it came to an end in quite an unexpected way.

One day excited rumors spread around the district: Jensen had been arrested with six young boys from the village. A patrol sent out by Captain Schnell had surrounded them in the forest where they were carrying on secret shooting practice, with Jensen as instructor and leader.

The military police had afterwards made a raid on the station and found a wireless set hidden in the ventilator in Jensen's room. He had to expect heavy punishment for this affair, perhaps even death.

The six young boys and their leader were sent to Oslo to be interrogated by the Gestapo. No one heard anything more of them that winter.

Ingrid and Elling were each full of the same thought: "What will happen to Stepan now?"

If they had been unwilling to talk to each other before, they were forced to do so now. Neither of them had to humble himself, for now they were concerned about someone other than themselves, someone in danger.

The day after the arrest they joined each other and walked home from school. It seemed to them quite natural to be talking again, and they immediately fell into the same confidential tone with each other that they had always had.

"Did Jensen tell you that he had meant to take Stepan to the frontier himself?" asked Elling.

"Yes. So now you and I alone are responsible for Stepan."

"I suppose so. We must think of something."

"Happily the Christmas holidays will soon be here. One of us must do it."

"Exactly. If we go then, it will make no one suspicious."

Ingrid made a face.

"And we shall need neither earache nor hospitals as an excuse, but we shall have to get a permit to travel by train, shan't we?"

"We'll forget that and trust to the conductor. Anyone mentioning Jensen's name will perhaps be allowed to travel free."

"That would be fine. Shall we draw lots?"

"What about?"

"About who shall go."

"Nothing to draw lots about," said Elling. "I know the way, and I am the strongest in case anything should happen."

Ingrid hesitated.

"I wonder if it is wise that you should travel the same way twice, Elling?"

"Wise? What do you mean?"

"We must try to imagine what Jensen would have said if he had been here to settle the matter."

"Oh, he'd have said, 'Off you go, Elling, the bolder the better!'"

"Not at all. Now I'll tell you what Jensen would have said: 'It's Ingrid's turn this time. Elling traveled this same way before and was no doubt noticed by many people on the road, both in Hamar, Elverum, and other places. Someone may become suspicious and will ask what this boy is doing wandering off toward the Swedish border again—'"

"This boy—what nonsense!"

"Now don't be offended, Elling, but listen to Jensen. He would have said, 'Ingrid will suit our purpose best. A sixteen-year-old girl does not arouse suspicion, not even with the border patrols. And then she is very good on her skis and can even hit people on the head, if necessary, or smile sweetly if that is more rewarding.'"

"Conceited fool!"

"Of course I'm conceited. But that's necessary, Jensen would say, if I'm to do the job properly."

"At any rate, you're far from stupid, Ingrid."

"You don't say! But you agree that Jensen would have said all that if he had been here?"

"Quite likely!" Actually Elling agreed, but he did not want to give in without a struggle.

"Good. Then I'll go," said Ingrid.

"Wait a minute—it's not settled yet. And besides, what would you tell your mother?"

"That I'm going to stay with a friend in Hamar. Bjørg in my class lives there in the holidays you see, and actually she has invited me to stay with her several times already."

"You're pretty smart, Ingrid!"

"There! You have to agree with me at last!"

"O.K., I give in."

Elling said this unwillingly, but in his inmost heart he was almost relieved. As he had already told Jensen, he did not particularly want any more of that sort of adventure. They walked on a few steps, talking over the plan.

"What do you think of Jensen?" asked Ingrid with a sudden tremor in her voice. "Do you think he will give anyone away when he is interrogated by the Gestapo?"

"Impossible to say. The best may crack under Gestapo interrogation. But I'm certain of one thing: no matter how much they torture Jensen, he'll never give Stepan away."

"No, I don't think he will. Besides, they may not ask him about that."

"No, he's been arrested for quite another matter. And I don't expect Captain Schnell will tell the Gestapo about Stepan, for they might perhaps laugh at a commandant who did not look after his prisoners better. I expect the Gestapo think of Stepan as just a little matter they don't want to bother about. And we all know that they're not very friendly with the officers in the Wehrmacht either."

"What a lot you've learned lately, Elling."

"Jensen told me a great many things when I lay hidden in his room."

"Jensen is a wonderful person. I hope they won't kill him!"

"Yes, Ingrid, we all hope that."

They were silent for a time. It was difficult to imagine that Jensen might be shot, almost as difficult as to imagine that they themselves might die, be stood up against a wall with German bayonets pointing at them. Such thoughts are impossible when one is only sixteen.

Elling turned to another subject.

"What will Teddy have to say if you go off?"

"Elling, you're jealous!"

"Not at all. I only thought it so absurd that you should hang about with that milksop."

"He's not like that when he's alone."

"He goes to the barber every Saturday and has his hair waved!"

"Do you envy him his lovely hair?"

"Nonsense, I'm not one of your good-looking chaps."

"No, happily not, Elling."

"But are you—are you in love with Teddy?"

"Not enough to matter. But you, Elling?"

"Yes?"

"Won't you tell me a little bit more about your trip with Stepan?"

"All right. Shall we go off to the café?"

"O.K."

25 — The Last Lap

Then came a time of ice cold air and strong frost at night. There was scarcely enough wood to heat the school, so the headmaster closed it for the Christmas holidays earlier than usual. On the first day of the holidays Ingrid went off with Bjørg to Hamar, fully equipped for a skiing expedition.

So this time it was Elling who had to stay at home and wait in uncertainty. The days passed, and he felt quite as lonely and nervous as had Ingrid. In imagination, he saw all the dreadful things that might happen to her and to Stepan. The possibilities were indeed many, for this last stage of the flight was often the most dangerous. The Germans kept a very close watch on the frontier districts and not a few fugitives met their fate in sight of the gate to freedom.

If they are caught now, it will be my fault, thought Elling gloomily. I ought not to have allowed Ingrid to take the job. He felt both deflated and depressed and more and more certain that something would go wrong.

Then one day the "report" reached him at last. It was quite different from anything he had imagined and was more or less as follows:

"I had to let Bjørg into part of the secret so that she knew the plan. Only just a very little, of course. I did not tell her who the refugee was or anything of that sort. Bjørg is entirely reliable. She was game immediately. She made inquiries and got me free transport in a truck over to Elverum. I had another plan ready in case anyone should have asked me for my frontier identification card. But no one did. I soon found Peter, who was very sweet to me, and very nervous about what was going to happen to Jensen. He drove me up to Stølen with a load of Christmas goods for the old people. There were two other fugitives with us, but they did not say a word all the way and hid their faces so that I might not see them. They disappeared like hares into the forest once we had arrived. Stepan shone like a summer sun when he saw me. He shouted hurrah and hugged me so violently that his false beard fell off. He was much better. He said that the old people had looked after him as if he had been a brigadier general at least. During the last few days they had been teaching him to ski. He was not exactly up to competition standard, but he managed to get along, and he was so full of courage and optimism that anyone might envy him. He sang both Norwegian and Russian patriotic songs when we started off. The Stølen folk had mapped out a sensible route for us. They thought that Stepan could not do it all in one stretch, so we were to spend the night in some fishing huts in the wilderness. That was a good plan because Stepan wore out his skis badly and fell every corner we came to, or so it seemed. I was terribly afraid that he would break a leg, but he smiled and laughed every time I had to drag him out of a snowdrift. He looked just like a snowman—even his hair and beard were full of snow. You should have seen us, Elling! We must have looked as comical as clowns many a time. But things went according to plan. We reached the fishing huts and even managed to sleep there. Keep calm, not in the same hut! We were out and away next morning at dawn. At midday the Swedish border guard came and met us. 'Hello,' he said, 'are you the only two today?' 'No,' said I, 'it's only one.' And then I did a right-about turn and here I am again, as you see."

Ingrid looked at Elling over the coffee table with her most coquettish smile. She had come back the day before Christmas Eve.

"Stepan sends you his love and thanks you for all you did," she told him. "He will be eating his Christmas dinner in Sweden just as Jensen promised." Her smile sent shivers of delight down Elling's back.

"Ingrid," he said, "do you know what Jensen would have said if he had heard what you have just been telling me? That you are the most courageous girl who has ever gone on skis across the Finn forest."

"Thank you—Jensen."

"And he would be just as glad as we are that Stepan has at last reached safety."

"I'm sure of that. What do you think they will do with him now?"

"He will be interned and will be given fine Swedish Christmas fare every day of the week, I imagine."

"And will not have to work with his spade and hoe? Then perhaps he'll have time to finish our present."

"That's an idea. Now that I think of it, he had some old metal in his pocket which he changed into his new clothes on the freight train. Perhaps that was the beginning of our present."

"Whatever can it be?"

"Don't you remember? A kind of box that will remind us two about—about—"

"About that we are in the same class at school," Ingrid finished, smiling. "But what could such a box look like?"

"We'll have to wait and see," said Elling.

26 — Stalingrad

After the New Year Captain Schnell gave up the hunt for Stepan. He did not take his revenge on the other prisoners, nor were any more shot or badly treated. Strangely enough, the starvation diet came to an end by degrees, the bread ration was increased by a few grams, and the soup water tasted a little more like soup.

The commandant did not march around the camp like a punishing tyrant any longer, the sentries were more careful about using the butts of their rifles on defenseless backs, and they did not force the sick out to work in the same way as before.

Slowly it seemed that a new and friendlier spirit toward the unfortunate prisoners was spreading among the guards. It seemed almost as if Captain Schnell had searched his conscience and discovered that he would like to become a better man. In fact, anyone who knew nothing of outside events might well have thought so. But those who followed the war news during this month of January, 1943, would have discovered a more likely reason for the commandant's new and surprising mildness: Captain Schnell was afraid of something. He was afraid of the war on the

Eastern Front, for things were going badly for the Germans in that region. More and more German troops were being taken prisoner by the Russians. Soon there would be as many German prisoners of war as there were Russians in German prison camps. The German prisoners could not expect to have better treatment than they had meted out to the Russians. This made Captain Schnell think again. He must no longer treat the Russian prisoners like beasts.

There was one word in the East that grew more and more important. It flew out on the waves of sound, out over the whole world, until it appeared like a giant specter before the eyes of the commandant and every German soldier wherever he was to be found: Stalingrad—the place where the war in Europe definitely took a turn and where the German defeat began that Jensen had foretold to the mayor.

When Jensen spoke of it in the autumn, the mayor had believed the lying propaganda that Stalingrad had fallen to the Germans. But now at last the propaganda men had to admit the truth: "Germany is living through the greatest trial in its history," they announced, and the posters saying, "Germany victorious on all fronts," were pulled down.

Early in February the Germans gave up their last resistance in Stalingrad. The Red Army shot victory salutes from many hundreds of cannons all at once. Germans all over Europe knelt in sorrow. Captain Schnell drank himself senseless.

Not long afterwards the mayor received a telephone call.

"Hello, is that the mayor?"

"Yes!"

"This is King Haakon. Congratulations on Stalingrad!" and then the connection was cut.

The mayor sat there with the receiver in his hand, feeling very strange. He had not recognized the voice on the telephone, but he guessed that it was one of Jensen's friends.

Why it almost seemed as if the man must have listened to that discussion about Stalingrad between Jensen and the mayor some time ago. Or perhaps Jensen had smuggled a greeting to him out of the concentration camp where he was now a prisoner.

The mayor did not know how it was all connected, but he could not lift a finger to find out. It was very difficult to function as an official, he thought, the way the war was going now.

27 — Stepan's Thanks

Stepan lay ill in a hospital in Sweden for a long time. The last part of his flight had used up more strength than he had to spare, and the Swedish military doctor who first examined him scarcely thought he would survive all his hardships. He suffered from pneumonia, undernourishment, overstrain, and serious digestive disorders, all at once.

But Stepan's will to live was stronger than all the learned prophecies. He had a firm aim in view that pulled him through weakness, fever, and dangerous operations. He wanted to send a "thank you" to all his helpers in Norway, a visible "thank you," a present he had made with his own artist's hands. He would not and could not go to the grave before he had done this. He clung fast to this aim with the whole strength of his will and so he survived, but weeks and months passed before he was allowed out of the hospital and could begin working seriously again with his hands.

He was very comfortable in the internment camp and was given as much material and as many tools as he needed. The work took a long time, for he would not let anything out of his hands unless it was absolutely flawless. Any object he made must be as perfect as he could possibly make it. There would be no careless work from Stepan.

So throughout the spring and summer, Stepan cut out his presents, filed them, polished them, and then polished again and again. There were many of these souvenirs, for he did not wish to forget anyone. Every person who had helped him in his flight was to have a gift to remember him by, a gift inspired by his own hand: Willie, Jensen, the conductor on the freight train, the old lineman and his wife, the timber driver Lars, Bergulv and Louisa, and all the others in that company, policeman Aslak in Hamar, the Hitler Youth boy who had gotten them onto the bus to Elverum (no doubt he would be very much surprised), Peter and his assistant, and that blessed good old pair at Stølen.

And finally, those two who were nearest Stepan's own heart—Ingrid and Elling. Now at last they were to receive the present he had promised them proudly over a year ago. The old people at Stølen had said that he could send everything to them and they would try and distribute the gifts to the right addresses.

One day in the autumn a secret courier from the Norwegian Legation in Stockholm went back to his fatherland with several strange things in his rucksack. He did not really understand what they were, for he was not used to carrying useless things across the border, but evidently they had all been made by an artist and were finely decorated. He was particularly interested in two little boxes. They were exactly alike but had an inscription in a strange code that he could not interpret.

One looked like this: And the other like this:

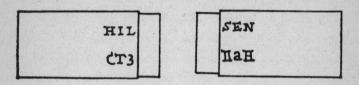

The courier had a great deal to do, but if he had had more time, he could perhaps have guessed how to put them together—for one fitted into the other. Then the "code" was clear, for the inscription, when translated, said: "Greetings, Stepan."

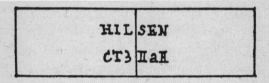

28 — Two in One

Stepan's double box took a long time to reach its goal.

Some of the others did the same—the one for Jensen, for instance, because he was in a concentration camp in Germany and was well on the way to becoming as starved and thin as Stepan had been in Norway. The gift to Peter never reached him: Peter was caught red-handed by the Gestapo and was shot in Akerhus fortress.

The two boxes reached their two recipients separately. Ingrid and Elling no longer lived in the same place, for they had finished all their examinations and Ingrid had moved to Oslo to continue her schooling there, while Elling took small jobs in the neighborhood of his home. He had come into contact with one of Jensen's foremost co-workers and eventually was given a very responsible job connected with the distribution of secret newspapers. Each of them hid the half box and looked at the meaningless half inscriptions, for they had to hide the gifts until the peace came—until the country was liberated in the wonderful spring of 1945—those weeks when a generous sun beat down on a Norway that had never been happier. It was the time when sorrow and revenge were drowned in a sea of freedom. Enemy soldiers disappeared, and friendly soldiers came and were received like princes and gods. Stepan's comrades from the prison camp were lent new Norwegian uniforms on which they put the Red Star so that they might take part in a victory parade beneath showers of flowers in Oslo. Of all the troops, they received the most flowers, for the spectators knew what they had suffered.

Jensen came home from Germany, together with only four of his fellow prisoners. He had developed tuberculosis and did not resemble very much the old gay telegraph clerk and Underground man. But he was alive and took part in the jubilation with all the powers he still had.

Ingrid's mother and Elling's mother went off to prepare their old houses against the time when their husbands should come home, *if* they came home, for no one knew yet whether their names figured in the long list of losses among Norwegian seamen.

Now the two halves of Stepan's box came out of their hiding places and were put together as Stepan had wished. The whole inscription became visible, and everyone could see what a wonderful box it was. After that no one ever thought of taking it apart.

And even to this day the box stands as a strange decoration on the mantelpiece in a certain house on the coast— in memory of Stepan and of the five dark years in Norway.